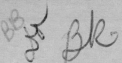 

"Don't go serious, Lyn. Life's meant to be fun!"

He stepped forward, and his arms closed around her. Lyn's heart thumped a wild tattoo of warning—or was it excitement?

"You have a need that must be fulfilled," Peter murmured huskily. "Don't stifle it. Let me teach you what it is to be loved."

Lyn shuddered under his touch. But it was not from pleasure. "It's not love, Peter," she said flatly. He was right; she did feel an ache, a terrible longing, but she knew she needed more than just a purely physical relationship.

"I'd do everything I could to please you." His voice was seductive, his personal magnetism hard to resist.

Her pulse raced disturbingly, but she shook her head. "I'm sorry, Peter. It's not enough. Trying out sex partners might be your way, but it's certainly not mine!"

Dear Reader,

This month we celebrate the publication of our 1000th Harlequin Presents. It is a special occasion for us, and one we would like to share with you.

Since its inception with three of our bestselling authors in May, 1973, Harlequin Presents has grown to become the most popular romance series in the world, featuring more than sixty internationally acclaimed authors. All of the authors appearing this month are well-known and loved. Some have been with us right from the start; others are newer, but each, in the tradition of Harlequin Presents, delivers the passionate exciting love stories our readers have come to expect.

We are proud of the trust you have placed in us over the years. It's part of the Harlequin dedication to supplying, contemporary fiction, rich in romance, exotic settings and happy endings.

We know you'll enjoy all of the selections in this very special month, and in the months to come.

Your friends at Harlequin

EMMA DARCY

the unpredictable man

Harlequin Books

TORONTO • NEW YORK • LONDON
AMSTERDAM • PARIS • SYDNEY • HAMBURG
STOCKHOLM • ATHENS • TOKYO • MILAN

Harlequin Presents first edition August 1987
ISBN 0-373-10999-7

Original hardcover edition published in 1986
by Mills & Boon Limited

CHAPTER ONE

LYN felt more isolated than ever. Her father sat next to her, driving the Daimler with taut concentration. From the back seat came a drone of soothing words as her mother tried to comfort Delvene, who was making certain that everyone knew how upset she was. No one had spoken to Lyn from the time they had all left the solicitor's office. They had looked at her as if she was an unwanted and distasteful insect ever since that astounding bequest had been read from Aunt Henrietta's will.

'She must have been mad!'

Alicia Mansfield stabbed the angry indictment towards her husband, but it was Lyn who felt the blow. The implication of the words was all too clear. Anyone who favoured Lyn over her beautiful sister, Delvene, must be mad. Tears pricked her eyes. Was it so unjust that for once in her life she had been favoured by someone? Just once? Years of experiencing her parents' rejection were still not armour enough against the hurt. The pain of loss sharpened. She would sorely miss her aunt, the only person in the Mansfield family who had ever treated her fairly. More than fairly in her will.

Lyn glanced apprehensively at her father to see his reaction to the suggestion of insanity in his sister. His face was grim, his eyebrows lowered in a frown of irritation. His hands tightened on the wheel of the Daimler as Delvene's dainty little hiccuping sobs grew marginally louder.

'There's no point in going on about it, Alicia,' he said tersely. 'The will is perfectly valid, and no court would uphold that the headmistress of the most prestigious girls' school in Sydney was of unsound mind. Apart from which I have no intention of dragging a family matter through the law courts. There has to be another solution. I'm sure this regrettable mistake can be settled fairly between ourselves.'

Lyn cringed even further. They would take the inheritance from her. Somehow. Some way. The car was now silent, and Delvene's sobs had stopped. Mission accomplished, Lyn thought bitterly. Delvene's tears invariably won whatever advantage she wanted. The back of Lyn's neck prickled. She could sense the vindictive hostility being shot at her by her sister, and feel waves of antipathy coming from all of them. A dull weariness settled on her soul.

It did not matter what she did; however hard she tried to be the daughter her parents wanted, Delvene always came first. More than ever Lyn felt shut behind the metaphorical door, refused entrance to the golden glow of approval which was always bestowed on Delvene. It still seemed incredible that Aunt Henrietta had actually favoured her, the ugly duckling of the Mansfield family.

Not that it would do her any good, she thought despondently. She was born a failure and bound to remain one, and there was nothing she could do about it. Aunt Henrietta had only made trouble for her in leaving her the beautiful home unit at Kirribilli.

The property was valuable, but to a wealthy establishment family like the Mansfields it did not mean so very much, except that it had come to Lyn. Everyone had received bequests in the will, but it was Lyn who had received the biggest jewel in the crown of Aunt Henrietta's estate, and that was unfair to Delvene. No one would have raised an eyebrow if Delvene had been the major beneficiary. That would have been the natural order of things, Lyn reflected wryly.

She didn't fit into this family. She was not cut out for the role of social butterfly, and she couldn't do anything right or look right or be right. Not like Delvene. Never like Delvene. It was no use even trying; she should give up trying and leave home.

Leave home. Leave home and do what she really wanted to do—make some success of her life instead of remaining the failure she would always be within the family circle. The idea took root and grew. Aunt Henrietta had given her a place to live completely apart from her family. If she could get a job ... any job would do, just to provide her with living expenses. She could use all her free time to work on her designs, and when Aunt Henrietta's will was probated and the money came through, she could open her own speciality shop and sell all that she had made. And with any luck get orders for more.

The rest of the trip home passed in a daze for Lyn. Her mind whirled with so many plans it didn't have room to worry about what her father or her mother or Delvene was thinking. As soon as the Daimler pulled to a halt Lyn was out and on her way up to her room, full of hopeful purpose.

A telephone call to the solicitor confirmed that she could indeed take up residence in Auntie's home unit whenever she liked. All she had to do was pick up the key from the solicitor's office. Which only left the problem of getting a job, and surely she could manage to obtain some employment. Her diploma from art school must be worth something to someone.

A wave of intense gratitude washed over Lyn's thoughts. She would never have gone to art school but for Auntie's intervention. Her father had declared art students scruffy, unconventional and socially questionable, and his daughter was not going to be one of them. Lyn's desire to pursue her interest had been crushed until Aunt Henrietta had waded into battle with her brother. It had not been an easy victory and Lyn might still have backed out of the issue but for Aunt Henrietta's stern eye on her, commanding that she should justify the support being given. Perhaps Auntie had meant the home unit to be another means of support. The idea warmed Lyn's heart and bolstered her resolve.

Even if the art school diploma couldn't get her a job she was well educated and knew how to present herself to her best advantage. She was prepared to accept just about any form of work. It was only a means to an end. It was the end that was all-important.

The ambition which had been squashed by her family's belittlement began to spark anew. Lyn opened her cupboards and dragged out the four huge plastic bags which stored her work. They represented the future she wanted, 'Lynette's little hobby', which would form the main stock of her speciality shop. She was about to open the bag which contained her favourite creation when Delvene walked in, unannounced and wearing a smirk on her perfect mouth.

'Well, Nettie, feeling pleased with yourself?'

The malicious gleam in the green eyes warned Lyn not to answer. She silently returned the plastic bags to their cupboard and locked the door on them. While her mother and father had consistently denigrated Lyn's art, Delvene had not been above getting her hands on anything she fancied, such as the sea-foam dress Lyn had designed and made for herself. 'Borrowing', Delvene called it, and her parents had let their beautiful daughter get away with it. But not any more, Lyn promised herself. Delvene was not going to take anything from her any more.

'Just out of interest, how did you persuade Auntie into leaving you the lion's share? I always thought you were too proud to beg or whine or tell tales, Nettie.'

Lyn eyed her sister warily. Delvene was lounging on the bed in a studied pose of feminine grace. 'I don't know why she did it and I had no idea she would,' she answered flatly.

'Straitlaced old bitch! She must have been mad.' Delvene never bothered with the virtuous air of sweetness and light when Lyn was the only audience. 'I'm glad she's dead,' she added vindictively. 'She always favoured you. Not that it'll do you much good, because Daddy's on my side.'

Lyn gritted her teeth. She felt like slapping Delvene but knew that would only rebound on herself. Instead she showed her contempt. 'Was she mad because she was the one person you couldn't curl round your little finger, Delvene? Is that how you judge people?'

Delvene smiled the smile of a smug feline about to pounce. 'Why, Nettie, you do have claws! But I wouldn't advise you to show them to Daddy. After all, Auntie is dead. She can't stand up and fight for you now, and a will is just a piece of paper, isn't it?' Her eyes glinted with malicious triumph. 'And by the way, Daddy wants to see you in the library for a private little chat. He told me to send you down to him immediately. The message just slipped my mind for a moment.'

Lyn's heart sank. A private chat with her father in the library meant only one thing; she was about to bear the brunt of his disapproval once again. With sick, dull eyes she watched Delvene swan out of her room, then, girding herself with renewed determination to leave all this behind her, she went downstairs to confront her father. For the last time.

She hated the library; it was the scene of too many hurts and defeats. She tried to calm her galloping pulse-rate and told herself to act and speak with calm dignity, no matter what her father said. When she entered the room he was standing propped against the desk, his arms folded, the usual frown for her on his face.

'I would be obliged not to be kept waiting in future, Lynette,' he snapped in irritation.

Past experience had taught Lyn there was no point in saying that anything was Delvene's fault. At his impatient wave she sat down in one of the huge leather chairs which always seemed to dwarf her slight frame, putting her at a psychological disadvantage. But she held on to her determination with a fierce will. She lifted her small, pointed chin to a defiant angle and fixed an unwavering gaze on her father.

He was a stolid man, still handsome at forty-nine, and still as blind as ever over Delvene. He cleared his throat portentously. 'Lynette . . . I've given this unfortunate matter my consideration. You realise, of course, that the will, as it stands, is grossly unfair to Delvene. I can't imagine what Henrietta was thinking of. I've decided that the home unit and its contents should be put on the market. The proceeds of the sale will be divided between you and your sister, as it should have been arranged in the first place.'

The blood drained from Lyn's face. Her dream of a life on her own, of her ambition being fulfilled, shimmered before her eyes. 'You can't do that,' she croaked uncertainly.

'Of course I can do it. All it needs is your signed agreement. Naturally I expect you to do the right thing over this, Lynette.'

The frown was even more beetling but Lyn steeled her backbone. 'No, Father, I won't do it. Auntie meant me to have her home unit and . . .'

He exploded with anger. 'Lynette! It's bad enough that you've gone behind our backs and influenced your aunt . . .'

Delvene's words! He always believed anything Delvene told him. Never once had he given Lyn the benefit of the doubt. Suddenly she was on her feet, trembling with all the bottled-up hurts of years. 'Is that what you truly think of me, Father? That I would even try to influence Auntie?'

'What else can I think?' her father thundered. 'It's unthinkable that Henrietta would slight Delvene in the normal course of events.'

Lyn swallowed the lump of painful emotion in her throat and spoke with more control, wanting, needing her father to listen to her point of view. 'I won't give up the home unit for Delvene! I'm going to live in it. I'll get a job and keep myself. And eventually I'll open a shop so that . . .'

'A shop!' he sneered contemptuously.

'Yes, a shop. It's what I want. You've never listened to what I want, Father. I need to . . .'

'I will not have a daughter of mine a common shopkeeper!' he shouted in self-righteous temper.

He wouldn't listen; he never had listened to her. Despair voiced her reply. 'Then disown me! I don't care any more. You might as well have disowned me years ago for all you cared about me.'

His face went red. 'I can't believe you said that, Lynette. You've had exactly the same love and attention and privileges as your sister.'

'Have I, Father? Exactly the same?' Lyn mocked bitterly.

His face went redder. 'Lynette, I find your jealousy of Delvene very unbecoming.' His voice rose to an insistent bluster. 'Give me one example! Just one example of this so-called favouritism!'

Lyn found his blindness too painful to keep fighting against it. She almost let the issue slide again, but it was the last time, the last chance she would ever have to open his eyes, and the need to reach her father still pulsed in her heart.

'I could give you a thousand examples, Father, but since you ask me for one, so be it.' With a few quick steps she reached the desk and picked up the gold-framed photograph which held pride of place. 'You and Delvene on her graduation night—the proud father and the beautiful daughter. Where's the photograph of you and me on my graduation night, Father?'

Tears swam into her eyes as she looked down at the photograph. The hurt was almost too much to bear. 'You took Delvene into the city and bought her the most beautiful dress you could find, and you were so proud of her you hired a photographer to come here and take this. You and your daughter.' The tears trickled down her cheeks as she looked up at her father. 'But you didn't do it for me.'

He cleared his throat and his reply was gruffly defensive. 'You didn't ask. All you had to do . . .'

'Delvene didn't have to ask,' she said sadly. 'I waited for you to offer. I waited for you to give me just a little of the love you've always showered on Delvene. I've been waiting too long, Father. I don't care any more whether you see me or not, but Delvene's had more than her share. I'm keeping Auntie's home unit and I'll be going in the morning. And nothing you can say now will change my mind.' She replaced the photograph and walked towards the door.

'Lynette! You come back here!'

She ignored the command and fled up to her bedroom. She felt too upset to stay and listen to her father defend himself, and she knew he would. Nothing was going to change and there was no more to be said. Her life in this house was over. She had already stayed too long, cocooned in a web of affluence, trying to be the daughter she would never be.

She began packing, thrusting all her possessions into suitcases and boxes until her room was stripped of everything that was hers. No one came to speak to her. Lyn knew that the arguments would come. This was only a respite. Delvene would not accept the loss and her father would inevitably want to please his darling daughter. As for her mother, Lyn was only too aware that she would never understand or accept Lyn's resolution to leave home, just as she had never tried to understand or accept her younger daughter's attitude towards anything.

It was in a mood of bleak resignation that Lyn went downstairs to dinner. Pride forbade that she should hide from the battle which would rage around her bid for independence, and she was as ready as she would ever be to resist all pressures.

One pressure was instantly removed. Delvene was bubbling over with high spirits. The injustice of Aunt Henrietta's terrible will had been more than redressed. Daddy was going to place an amount of money equal to Lyn's inheritance in Delvene's account tomorrow, to be frittered away as she pleased.

'In the interests of fairness,' Gerald Mansfield declared pointedly.

Delvene's eyes were glinting with smug glee, and Lyn glanced at her mother. The older version of Delvene's beautiful face was coldly set in condemnation of her younger daughter. Lyn's resolution firmed. She looked her father straight in the eye and spoke with bitter irony.

'I don't know what's fair or not any more, Father.

I just know there's no place in this family for me.'

His mouth thinned. 'I'm disappointed in you, Lynette. I would have thought you'd had time to get over your temper tantrum and be reasonable. Since I can't force you to sign over what is legally yours, I hope you'll have sense enough to see that Henrietta's home unit can give you a useful income. It's ridiculous to talk of leaving home.'

'Nevertheless I'm going, Father. I've spoken to Auntie's solicitor, and it's perfectly all right for me to take possession of the home unit tomorrow. I'm leaving in the morning,' Lyn stated with flat determination.

'You can't go, Lynette!' her mother spluttered. 'What will people think? Gerald, she can't go.'

'If you go, Lynette, don't expect me to support you,' he warned tersely.

Lyn held her father's gaze, not wavering a millimetre. 'Don't you know it was never money that I wanted from you?' she asked sadly.

He frowned, yet it was not the usual frown of disapproval. For the first time it seemed that his eyes were opened to the pain she had suffered under his blindness. The frown deepened. He opened his mouth as if to speak, then shut it again, shaking his head in some confusion of mind.

His wife suffered no such confusion. She broke the short silence with positive command, cutting the tenuous link between Lyn and her father. 'I won't put up with it, Lynette! I will not have you going off and doing things which will ruin your social standing. It's ungrateful and ... and eccentric, to say the least.'

'Oh, Mummy!' Delvene soothed indulgently.

'Nettie's over twenty-one. Let her try it on her own for a while.'

Lyn's hidden grimace was full of irony. Of course Delvene would only be too happy to take her side. It suited her very well to be the only daughter of the house. As for her mother, Lyn knew her only concern was for what 'others would think'. That had always been her first and only concern, the one rule by which everything was measured.

'But she'll be living next door to *that man*,' her mother said with pronounced distaste. 'It's not the place for a respectable girl. It was all right for Henrietta, no one could point a finger at an elderly spinster, but Lynette's good name will definitely be at risk.'

Delvene laughed, a delicate little tinkle of derision. 'Stop worrying, Mummy. Peter Kelso probably won't even notice that Nettie's there.'

'You miss the point, Delvene,' her mother declared waspishly. 'The sheer proximity could give rise to unpleasant gossip.'

'Oh, Mummy! Nettie is hardly news material. Think of the women he's been linked with. They've all been big-name personalities or real stunners.'

That's right, rub it in, Delvene. The ugly duckling of the Mansfield family was most unlikely to draw the interest of such a notorious womaniser.

'The Mansfield name is always news,' Alicia Mansfield stated with ingrained snobbery. 'And *that man* has no respect for names. It would probably amuse him to drag ours through the mud. Look what he did to the Thursons!' Her voice took on a mournful tone. 'They'll never be able to hold up their heads in society again.'

'A stockbroker shouldn't embezzle, Mummy,' Delvene said with sweet virtue.

'I'll never be convinced that Howard Thurson wasn't investing on behalf of his clients. If it hadn't been for that ... that gambler ...' Alicia frowned at her silent husband. 'And I still think it's disloyal of you to subscribe to his financial newsletter, Gerald. The Thursons were one of us.'

'The advice is always sound, that's why,' came the flat answer. 'And a man who's made millions by ...'

'Gambling!' His wife's interjection was coated with contempt.

'We all gamble, Alicia, every time we make a new investment,' came the uninterested retort.

And that's what I'm doing, Lyn thought with satisfaction. Making a new investment in my life.

But her mother was not satisfied. She huffed with exasperation. 'Gerald! You can't possibly approve of Lynette's going to live next to him. His reputation is shocking, sordid. You can't turn a blind eye to that. Peter Kelso is nothing but a ... a scoundrel and a roué. And I will not stand for any daughter of ours being remotely connected to him. It's unthinkable!'

Her father's gaze turned to Lyn. There was a struggle to understand in his eyes, but the struggle was hurting in ways he had not expected. 'Lynette, your mother has a valid point,' he said more tentatively than he had ever spoken to her.

For a moment Lyn hesitated, wanting to reach out for the understanding she had always yearned for. Maybe his heart and mind were open enough for her to get through to him. But Delvene was there

and her presence was too inhibiting. Lyn glanced at
her. The faint smirk on her sister's perfectly shaped
mouth promised that any such opening would soon
be shut again. It was too late now anyway. Far, far
too late.

'You should have faith in the Mansfield upbringing, Father. I've had twenty-three years of it, and
we never have been encouraged to be familiar with
neighbours, have we?'

And in truth, she had no intention of mixing with
the notorious man who would be her new neighbour, but she could not deny her interest was stirred.
In all her visits to her aunt she had never met him.
Undoubtedly Aunt Henrietta had deemed him an
unsuitable acquaintance, even in passing. However, Lyn was bound to run into him sooner or later
since they would be sharing the same floor of the
apartment building.

Alicia Mansfield, meanwhile, was not in the least
mollified by any faith in Lynette's upbringing. Her
husband's failure to back up her arguments was no
deterrent, and for once she dismissed Delvene's
sweet soothing. Her nagging disapproval continued
the next morning, becoming more and more
personal as Lyn kept packing her possessions into
her estate car. It was difficult to ignore the torrent of
shrill abuse, but Lyn determinedly kept her temper.
She had said all she was going to say.

Delvene put in a diplomatic appearance on the
farewell scene. Lyn fixed a smile on her mouth and
gave her mother a perfunctory kiss on the cheek.
''Bye now, Mother.'

She turned to her father, who had helped her with
the heavy luggage in grim silence. He had said no

word against his wife's tirade, but neither had he joined his voice to hers in disapproval or protest. Lyn met eyes which were disturbingly troubled.

'Goodbye, Father. Thank you for all you've done for me.'

He took her hand as she was about to turn away and squeezed it in some agitation of feeling. 'You will come to me if you need anything, Lynette,' he said in a gruff voice.

Could she? No, Lyn decided sadly. That time was past, buried underneath all the refusals to listen, the blindness to see, the love which had never been expressed in real terms. Regret for all the lost opportunities softened her voice. 'I'll remember that, Father.'

Her gaze traversed the Mansfield mansion one last time before she stepped into the car. A huge, impressive edifice, a veritable institution, a magnificent house. It had never been a home to her.

She settled into the car, closed the door, started the engine, and set off down the tree-lined driveway without a backward glance. Behind her lay the past, and it saddened her too much to dwell on those heart-sickening failures. She did not regret her decision. The future beckoned . . . a clean slate on which she would write her own destiny.

CHAPTER TWO

LYN pressed the door shut behind her and stood against it, quite still, hardly breathing as her eyes danced round the apartment, drinking in all there was to be seen. All hers. The sense of freedom was intoxicating, the sense of utter privacy even more so. And there was so much room, so much lovely, luxurious room to move in, to live in, to work in, to be herself in.

She stepped away from the door and gave vent to her elation in a few mad pirouettes before dashing through the rooms, whisking curtains aside and throwing windows open. The bright sunshine poured in, lifting her spirits even higher. Unable to resist the attraction of the balcony which ran the length of the living-room, Lyn stepped outside and leaned on the railing, hugging herself in sheer delight.

The view was superb. On her right was the Sydney Harbour Bridge. Directly opposite her was the Opera House with its roof of sails gleaming in the bright sunshine, and below, stretching out to sea, was a sparkling expanse of water, busy with the interesting traffic of an international harbour. And this too was hers, whenever she wanted to look at it.

Her home. Her very own home, she exulted as she turned back inside, but as her gaze rested more critically on Aunt Henrietta's décor she adjusted that thought. Not quite her home . . . yet. When she could afford it, she would furnish it to her own taste, replacing the neutral colours and ladylike furniture with something more vibrant and alive. Like her lovely bedspreads.

Lyn sighed with pleasure at the thought that they would no longer have to be packed away, hidden from critical or coveting eyes. The two spare bedrooms could be turned into workrooms where everything could be left spread out for her to pick up or put down as she chose. And tonight ... tonight she could sleep under her favourite creation. That would put the colour she loved into the master bedroom.

Eager to get settled in, she took the two small suitcases she had brought up with her into the bedroom she would occupy. Her mind was busy planning where she would put everything as she changed out of the clothes she had worn to visit the solicitor's office. Then, coolly dressed in brief lemon shorts and sun-top, she took the lift down to the basement garages and started unpacking the car in earnest.

She lugged the two largest suitcases over to the lift and was relieved to let them go and press the button for her floor. She watched the numbers tick over on the slow ascent to the top floor. Every other floor held four apartments, but there were only two at the top, hers and *that man's*.

Lyn grinned to herself over her mother's reluctance even to acknowledge his name. Whether his reputation was well-earned or not, Lyn decided he couldn't be a troublesome neighbour or Aunt Henrietta wouldn't have put up with him for ten years. The lift slid to a halt. The doors rolled open, and Lyn was already bending to grab the handles of the suitcases when her eyes registered that her way out was comprehensively blocked.

Two hands were roving familiarly over a well-rounded bottom. Lyn's startled gaze lifted higher. There were certainly no inhibitions about this clinch. Even from the back view the blonde's curves suggested she was cheesecake material. The face and the figure of her partner in passion were obscured, but there could be no doubt about his identity.

Lyn did not know what to do. Embarrassment mixed with resentment that she should be subjected to such a display. Those hands were disgustingly busy. In public view too! It was one thing to hear about a man like this, quite another to see him in action—and intimate action at that! Only the fact that he probably thought he still had the floor to himself mitigated the offence.

Lyn decided that cool dignity was the only way to carry off the situation. Doing her best to pretend indifference to the impassioned farewell, she leaned against the back wall of the lift, folded her arms and waited.

'Now, promise you'll be there,' came the breathy command from the blonde.

'Jessie ...' The weary drawl denied any promises.

He would avoid promises like the plague, Lyn surmised.

'Well, try then.'

Lyn imagined the sexy pout, and a grimace of distaste curved her own lips down as she straightened up, ready to move. Her gaze lifted expectantly and found a pair of brown eyes dancing their amusement at her. Lyn stared back in surprise. She had assumed he would be handsome, but she wouldn't even call his face particularly attractive, let alone handsome. How had he got all those beautiful women into his bed?

'Jessie, Miss Mansfield has very kindly kept the lift waiting for you and you're already running late. As for this afternoon, I'll see how I feel. Off you go now.' With a slap on the rump which was both playful and authoritative, he turned the blonde away from him. Then he swooped forward, grabbed Lyn's two suitcases and lifted them out of the way.

Jessie threw him a little moue of reproof before stretching her lips into a dismissive smile for Lyn. 'Thanks. You're a sweetie.'

'That's all right,' Lyn murmured, unable to keep a faint note of derision out of her voice. She quickly moved aside so that the woman could step into the lift. The blonde might not have much in the line of conversation, but she was certainly well stacked and every ample curve undulated as she walked. Lyn could not check a little stab of envy. In comparison her own slight figure was almost boyish, a zero register in the sensuality stakes.

The lift doors closed on a beautiful toothpaste smile directed at lover-boy. Lyn glanced round, expecting to see a fatuous response on his face. He was leaning against her doorjamb, clothed in nothing more than a bathrobe and observing her with amused interest.

'So, I'm not much to look at and you're not a sweetie,' he mocked softly, his mouth gradually widening into a huge grin. 'How do you do, Miss Mansfield?'

His accurate reading of her expressions totally disarmed Lyn. After a moment of sheer surprise she found herself grinning back. 'Oh, I manage in my own small way, but I'm obviously not a match for you, Mr Kelso,' she replied, returning his mockery with a nod towards the lift.

He chuckled and straightened up. His physique was impressive and all too obvious since the short, wrap-around robe had become less wrapped around in the clinch with the blonde. An expanse of broad chest held a sprinkling of dark curls. His arms and legs had the strong muscularity of a boxer, and indeed his face had the battered look of a man who had spent some time in the ring.

His skin was deeply tanned and his straight black hair flopped on to his rather low forehead, giving him a raffish air. If he had had a moustache to go with his large ears, Lyn decided he would look a little like the Clark Gable she had seen in *Gone With The Wind*.

She suddenly realised her appraisal was being returned in full measure. In a self conscious flurry she fished in her pocket for the door key.

'For a good sensible girl, you have a lovely pair of legs.'

The unexpected compliment increased Lyn's self consciousness. She was not used to compliments about her body. No one even saw her body when Delvene was around, and she didn't want a type like Peter Kelso noticing it now. He probably handed out lines like that to every woman, she reasoned, annoyed with herself for feeling even momentarily pleased. She found the key and favoured him with a look of arch scepticism. 'Pity about the face.'

'Yours or mine?'

It drew a wry smile from her. 'I was born with mine. What happened to yours?'

He shrugged and moved aside to let her unlock the door. 'I guess you could say life happened to it. The nose got rearranged in a water-skiing accident. I had an argument with a tree when sky-diving. And age does tend to leave its scars year by year. But I'm perfectly comfortable with what I've got.' He slid her a measuring look. 'What's your complaint?'

He had been studying her as he spoke and Lyn was all too aware of what he was seeing. A good hairdresser had made the most of her mousey hair, shaping the coarse thickness into a becoming cap and tinting it a rich auburn. The style accentuated her rather elfin features, but Lyn had decided that since she had to live with them she might as well play up their dubious attraction.

Her heart-shaped face was out of balance, the high, wide forehead and high cheekbones curving too quickly to her delicately pointed chin. The hazel eyes were too large, and although they were fringed with long, thick eyelashes, these only served to make her eyes look even larger in what was a small face. Her tip-tilted nose was passable enough and her mouth was nicely shaped, although a fraction wider would have been helpful. Then there were her ears. Slightly pointed and completely lobeless, they, more than anything, had earned her the nickname of Pixie while she was at school. But at least they were tucked close to her head, she consoled herself.

A classical beauty she was not, and never could be. Not like Delvene.

She thrust the door open wide and turned to him with a dismissive smile. 'I'll put it this way. My face is not exactly my fortune, is it?'

'I like it. It has individuality,' he declared with authority.

'It certainly has that.'

His eyes narrowed. 'I find it interesting.'

Lyn suddenly recalled the shrewd perception of the man and wished she had not revealed so much about herself by making those last few comments. Peter Kelso would not have missed their implications.

'You're very kind, Mr Kelso,' she said drily, dismissing him as she bent down to pick up her suitcases.

He forestalled her, his bathrobe falling perilously agape as he leaned over and took possession of them. 'I've barely begun to be kind to you, Lynette.'

'Lyn,' she corrected automatically.

'Peter,' he smiled, and it was a soft, warm, genial smile which held no trace of depravity.

'I don't need help,' Lyn said quickly, trying once more to dismiss him.

'Nonsense—these are heavy. Besides, I like playing the benevolent Samaritan to good sensible girls.'

And while Lyn was too bemused to stop him he strode past her into the living-room, through the living-room and straight into the master bedroom. He strolled back as if he was entirely at home.

'Do you have some inbuilt instinct for finding a woman's bedroom?' she remarked acidly.

He laughed, not at all piqued by the observation. 'I'm not quite so dependent as that on the female sex, but they do provide splendid exercise. Some people play squash to keep fit; others play golf or tennis or work out at a gym. I prefer sex—much more pleasurable and often more strenuous. I'd recommend it to anyone. Shall we get on with the unloading?'

While Lyn was still swallowing her shock over his shameless profligacy he added affably, 'Lucky I caught up with you so soon. You have, of course, more than a few suitcases of possessions.'

Lyn nodded dumbly, then found her voice. 'You don't intend to help me dressed like that?' she choked out.

He glanced down at the offending bathrobe. 'What's wrong with this? It's very comfortable.' He cocked a quizzical eyebrow at her. 'Matter of fact, I'm more covered up than you are. Not that I'm complaining. All women like to show off what they've got. For which I'm extremely grateful—it always gives me pleasure to watch the female form in action. And yours I'm finding particularly delightful.'

And with that comment he ambled past her and over to the lift to summon it once more. Lyn stared after him, not knowing whether to be outraged or amused. She had never met such an eccentric character before, or such a blatantly wicked one. Not someone a good, sensible girl should get involved with at all. The phrase tickled her mind.

'Why did you call me a good sensible girl?' she asked curiously. 'You don't even know me.'

He grinned at her, the brown eyes full of

devilment. 'Your aunt's description. But Old Henry was not one for delving deeply.'

Old Henry! That was the name the girls at school had given Aunt Henrietta, the straitlaced headmistress who had run the Presbyterian College for Young Ladies with undeviating moral authority. But for this man ... 'You didn't ever call my aunt Old Henry to her face?' she asked in flat disbelief.

'She loved it.'

Lyn shook her head. 'I don't believe you.'

He chuckled, amused by her incredulity. 'Oh, she sniffed the first few times, but having been called Old Henry behind her back for thirty years, I think she quite enjoyed being actually faced with it. It was a term of affection, you know. We were very close friends. In fact, the last thing she said to me before she died was, "Look after Lynette", and I gave her my solemn promise to do so. She was very concerned about you.'

Lyn was flabbergasted. 'Concerned?'

He nodded. 'Said your family was stifling you. That's why she changed her will in your favour.'

The lift doors opened, and with a slightly mocking sweep of the arm he invited her to step in. Lyn no longer thought of refusing. Incredible as it seemed, Peter Kelso had obviously enjoyed Aunt Henrietta's confidence, and Lyn was far too curious to turn away from him now. She joined him without another word.

He pressed the down button and leaned back against the side-wall of the compartment, eyes watching her with speculative interest. Very deliberately she moved to the opposite wall, facing him with her own speculative interest. He grinned at the manoeuvre as if it pleased him, which irritated Lyn, since she had apparently done what he wanted.

'You must have known Aunt Henrietta very well,' she remarked more sharply than she had meant to.

The grin softened to a rueful smile. 'We were friends. In the truest and closest sense of the word.'

Lyn couldn't accept that. Aunt Henrietta had surely disapproved of Peter Kelso. It would have been totally out of character for a woman of her moral principles to look kindly upon such a flagrant womaniser. As for walking around in his bathrobe and nothing else, in public view . . . her aunt's icy stare would have cut him in half.

'I don't believe it. You were poles apart—nothing in common at all.' A mocking little smile curled her mouth. 'If my mother could see me with you now, she'd be scandalised out of her mind. For you to say that my aunt, who was even more 'proper' than my mother, asked you to take care of me . . .' She shook her head in flat disbelief.

The lift bumped to a halt and Lyn stepped forward expectantly. The doors rolled open, but before she could move a hand fell heavily on her shoulder and gripped hard. Bristling with rejection, she glared up at Peter Kelso. There was no teasing amusement on his face; it was deadly serious and his eyes bored into hers.

'Things aren't always what they appear,' he said softly, yet his voice carried a grim authority. 'I've spent my life searching for the ultimate, the best. All that is rare, unique, different, special. And of all I've experienced, people are the most disappointing.'

His fingers dug into her soft flesh, lending emphasis to his speech. 'And of all the people I've met, your aunt held more of the qualities for which I seek than any other person. I treasured her. My life is all the more barren for her loss. You didn't know her, Lyn.'

He released her shoulder and stepped out, shrugging off his serious mood and throwing a teasing smile back at her. 'If you can even come near to filling her shoes it would be some consolation. Meanwhile the search goes on.'

Lyn felt hopelessly confused. She followed him to the car, her mind struggling to grasp the essence of the man. What had he said? 'Things aren't always what they appear.' If he had truly been a close friend of Aunt Henrietta, then maybe he wasn't the terrible womaniser of his reputation. Perhaps he simply enjoyed shocking people. The man was totally unpredictable, full of contradictions.

But she had seen him in action with Jessie. Surely that was evidence of a rapacious appetite. And she resented the suggestion that he had known Aunt Henrietta better than she had. Apart from the family association, Lyn had attended her aunt's school for six years, listening to her lectures and edicts, experiencing at first hand the whole sum of her philosophy of life. And that philosophy was against everything Peter Kelso stood for.

A memory suddenly slotted into place. As she unlocked the car, Lyn arched a sceptical eyebrow at Peter Kelso. 'I'm sorry I didn't know my aunt as well as you obviously did, but I think you're deluding yourself over her opinion of you. I can tell you precisely what she thought of you.'

He grinned, not at all perturbed. 'And what was that?'

'She said you were a genius and a fool. A genius for what you were capable of doing and a fool for what you did,' Lyn recited with considerable satisfaction.

He cocked his head as if running the words over in his mind, checking them against his own knowledge. 'She said that?' he queried with something suspiciously like delight.

'Yes, she did,' she assured him with slightly less satisfaction.

The satisfaction had changed hands. 'You see? She liked me in spite of herself. I must see my solicitor tomorrow,' he added with relish.

Lyn was lost. 'Whatever for?'

'I want those words to be my epitaph when I die. Now, if you'll unwind this rear window, we can start getting the luggage out.'

He had done it again—surprised her into losing track of what she was supposed to be doing. With an exasperated sigh at herself Lyn pressed the button to unwind the window.

Peter lowered the tailgate of the car and began sliding out boxes. As Lyn picked up her first load she noticed he was frowning, as if displeased with the task he had set himself. He worked without comment, transferring her goods to the lift with speedy efficiency. The face whose expressions had been so mobile and provocative now seemed to be shuttered against her. Lyn was puzzled by the cooling of his interest. She wondered if she had offended him after all, although his conversation had not suggested any acrimony.

She tried to shrug off her disquiet. It was no skin off her nose if Peter Kelso chose to distance himself. He was not the type of man whose interest she wanted. It was only his assertions about a friendship with her aunt which had intrigued her, but if he no longer wanted to speak to her, that was fine. It was not as if she had even asked for his help; he had thrust it upon her, overriding her protests.

Nevertheless his silence piqued her. There was a slight air of contempt about it which she did not understand at all. And what right did he have to be contemptuous of her? Lyn was glad when the last load had been carried into her apartment and there was no longer any reason for his unwanted company.

She switched on a polite smile. 'Thank you so much. It was very kind of you to help.'

He straightened up from propping the last two plastic bags against a box and gave her a look of faint derision. 'Well, I hope Old Henry isn't turning in her grave!'

It was some kind of dig at her and Lyn frowned over it. 'Why should she? My moving in here couldn't be against her will.'

His mouth curled to one side. 'You know why Old Henry made that will, Lyn? She told me you had more artistic talent in your little finger than she'd seen from anyone else in her whole teaching career. She thought your family was stifling your talent and she wanted to free you from their influence.' His hand made a mocking sweep of her possessions. 'Yet I see no easel, no canvases, no ...'

'I don't paint!' Lyn bit out, resenting the

implication that she was failing to live up to her
aunt's judgement.

One eyebrow rose in polite interest. 'Oh?'

'There are other forms of art,' she remarked
acidly. 'And you've just been carrying my work, as
it happens.'

His gaze dropped to the plastic bags and Lyn was
pleased to see him puzzled for once.

'Tapestries?'

'No, not tapestries.' Lyn stepped forward and
hoisted up the bag which held her best design. 'You
just wait here—I'll show you. And then you can
apologise.'

Without giving him the chance of reply she
strode into the master bedroom, unfastened the bag
and slid it off the carefully rolled bedspread. She
lifted the heavy spread on to the bed, unrolled it,
and removed the tissue paper. Then she adjusted
the positioning of the bedspread so it was displayed
to its best advantage. She stood back to survey it
with possessive pride before calling Peter Kelso in.

Only then did doubts attack her confidence.
What if he wasn't impressed? Every self-protective
instinct shied away from inviting criticism. If Peter
Kelso belittled her art, her sense of purpose would
be badly shaken. On the other hand, it was stupid to
hide her head in the sand. Either her work was
saleable or it wasn't, and Peter's reaction to it
should be some gauge to judge by.

She took a deep breath and called him in. Her
need for approval was so intense that she completely forgot that a bedroom was the last place where
any good sensible girl should ever invite Peter
Kelso.

CHAPTER THREE

LYN moved to one side as Peter entered the bedroom. Nervous tension cramped her stomach. She ignored his presence, telling herself that his opinion did not matter. She fixed her gaze on the bedspread, assuring herself she was not mistaken as to its art value.

The sunrise over mountains had been the most dramatic of her designs and she loved it—the purple and midnight-blue velvet of the mountains, the huge, golden satin sun, the pale blue and mauve strips of sky, the lemon and pink clouds of silk, and the darker velvet sky above, balancing the mountains. Of course it did not suit this room, Aunt Henrietta's mushroom carpet and lace curtains were hardly the furnishings to highlight this bedspread, but to Lyn's mind they were cancelled out by the riveting dominance of this one work of art.

It was good. She knew it was good. Surely Peter Kelso could not say it was anything else but good? But despite her own confident judgement, she could not bring herself to look at him. Her heart was thudding painfully against a constricted chest. She waited, her mind suddenly seething with doubts as he remained silent.

He moved forward, into her range of vision. His head was shaking in a seemingly negative fashion, and Lyn bit her lip, forcing back an instinctive cry of protest. His hand reached out and slowly slid across the different fabrics, lingering on each join to feel the change of texture.

When he straightened up and looked directly at her, the dark eyes held a strangely distant expression, as if they were considering her from another dimension. His mouth slowly curved into a bemused smile. 'Extraordinary,' he murmured.

A nervous laugh gurgled out of Lyn's throat before she grasped the presence of mind to say, 'Well, it has to be extraordinary if I'm to command an exclusive price.'

He grinned. 'What's your price? You can sell it to me right now.'

She laughed the free, open laugh of relief. He liked it so much that he wanted to buy it. 'Sorry, but it's not for sale. I made this one for myself.'

His mouth quirked to one side. 'And there won't be any copies.'

'No.'

'What price do you intend to ask for such work?'

She shrugged off her disquiet and answered matter-of-factly. 'I thought, maybe fifteen hundred dollars.'

'It's too cheap,' he said slowly, deliberately, his expression one of reflective consideration. 'You could get four or five thousand. I'd certainly pay that sum for this one. If you change your mind . . .'

'Would you really?'she asked, wondering if it was feasible to ask such a price.

'Then you'll sell it?'

'No, I told you it's not for sale.'

'Yet I want it,' he said very deliberately, and the tone of his voice seemed to curl around her, compulsively acquisitive, suggesting desire which had no experience of being refused. 'I'll give you ten thousand for it.'

She stared at him incredulously. 'You're mad!'

'Not at all. Does ten thousand buy it?'

'It's not for sale,' she repeated irritably. Was he so used to getting his own way that he thought he could buy everything?

He cocked his head on one side. His face looked oddly taut as if every muscle was concentrated on one purpose and that purpose glittered in his eyes. 'Still not enough to tempt you? I do like possessing unique things. What about twenty thousand, Lyn?'

She shook her head, frowning at his persistence. Couldn't he accept that she didn't want to sell it? It was hers. Her first really satisfying creation, and nothing would persuade her to part with it.

'Fifty thousand.'

'Oh, for God's sake! That's ridiculous!' she burst out impatiently.

'I'll get my chequebook.'

'No, you won't! It's mine. It's part of me. It'd be like selling myself. It wouldn't matter what price you're willing to pay, I wouldn't give it up. You can't have it, not for all the money in the world!'

The hard glitter in his eyes glowed into an approving warmth. His facial muscles relaxed as his mouth quirked into a whimsical little smile. 'You're right—integrity is priceless. I can see you'll have to give it to me as a gift. So then, let it be a gift, from you to me.'

Lyn huffed her exasperation. 'I wouldn't bet on that ever happening.'

'I'm a gambler, Lyn, with a lot of wins to my credit.'

The devilish twinkle in his eyes was oddly discomfiting. She had the distinctive feeling that he was talking about more than bedspreads. His fingers trailed once more across the fabrics, seemingly fascinated by each change of texture. Lyn smiled her understanding. She loved the feel of the fabrics too. The touch of them gave her as much pleasure as their visual impact.

'Beautiful and sensual,' Peter Kelso murmured as his eyes lifted to hers, and something in their depths, something distinctly predatory, caused a weird jiggle in her heart.

He meant her work—of course he meant her work. He couldn't possibly mean he considered her, the ugly duckling of the Mansfield family, beautiful and sensual. 'Would you like to look at the others I've made?' she asked.

'I'd like to see everything you have,' he replied softly.

Lyn looked hard at him, suspecting a double entendre, but his smile of limpid innocence disarmed her. She fetched her folder of designs for him to look through while she unpacked the other three bedspreads. His comments on her sketches revealed a knowledgeable appreciaton of line and colour, as well as a keen sense of the drama and subtleties of each pattern.

No one, except her teachers, had ever concentrated such intense interest on her work, and Lyn found the experience heady and intoxicating. However, she felt a little stab of disappointment when he did

not offer to buy either the second, third or fourth
bedspread she displayed.

'These last three are for sale,' she prompted.

'And will sell well,' he assured her with a knowing
smile. 'They're exquisite, unique. But nothing
you've shown me surpasses the first. That has
passion.'

Lyn almost bridled with pleasure. 'Once I have
enough stock I'm going to open a shop,' she
confided.

Peter gave her a curious look. 'You're being
shortsighted. It would be tying yourself to unnecessary overheads. Channel your work through an
interior decorator. I could name half a dozen who'd
be banging on your door, begging you to let them
put such unique creations on display. These are
prestige items.'

Lyn hadn't thought of that. Her mind had been
stuck on a shop of her own. But she did not have any
experience at wheeling and dealing, and she
instinctively shrank from the idea of trying to push
her work on to an established outlet. 'I don't think I
can do that,' she said uncertainly.

He eyed her with an uncomfortable degree of
speculation. 'Better for you not to. An artist can
never properly value her own work. You need an
agent.'

'You?' she asked hopefully. Just his air of
supreme confidence would probably win Peter
Kelso an ear to the most unlikely proposition.

He shook his head slowly. 'Not my game. But I
can introduce you to the right people. Why not try
it? Think of the advantages.'

She shook her head. She didn't really like the idea

of relying on other people. And they always took advantage of you. She had had too much bitter experience of being let down too many times.

'I'll set it up for you,' he prompted persuasively.

Lyn eyed him with suspicion. Such an offer was extraordinarily generous. People didn't give their time and efforts for nothing. 'Why should you do that for me? What's in it for you?'

'Pleasure,' he drawled softly, and smiled, a slow, provocative smile.

Shock pummelled Lyn's heart. God! Those evocative words he had used ... they had held double meanings. And he had the arrogance to stand there, smiling at her like a spider that had cleverly enmeshed his quarry!

Lyn could feel herself going red and she completely lost her temper, flinging her arms out in a rage of disgust as she spat her contempt. 'You lecher! Anyone's grist to your sordid sexual treadmill, aren't they? Well, not me, neighbour, so go peddle your bed elsewhere and stay out of my way!'

He chuckled. Her eyes stabbed revulsion at him, but he kept on chuckling. 'What a low view you have of sex, Lyn! The most exquisite act of pleasure between a man and a woman, and you apply such nasty words to it. Shame on you!'

He strolled towards her, his grin teasing the outrage still stamped on her face. 'But you underestimate me. I enjoy pleasures—many of them. And right now I'm enjoying the pleasure of having discovered an exciting new talent.' He stopped in front of her and his eyes gently mocked the rigid reserve in hers. 'I don't like to see time and effort wasted, particularly when that time and effort could be spent in creating what you have the talent to create.'

Lyn felt wretchedly confused. Had she misjudged the man? No, not entirely. Every instinct was registering the strong sexuality being projected by Peter Kelso. He was so aggressively male, so assured, so completely in control . . . and she was a mess of uncertainties.

Then suddenly there was no mockery in his eyes, but a deep respect which seeped into her barren, lonely soul and gave root to a flower of extraordinary sweetness. 'You're very special, Lyn,' he murmured, his voice a silky caress. 'Far too special to be ensconced behind a counter. You should be free to express yourself in the way that only you know. It would give me great pleasure to know that I set you free.'

Lyn was mesmerised by that soft reverence. It was more addictive than the most powerful drug. And the words, heady, hypnotic words. To be set free. A hand gently cupped her cheek, a thumb swept a light caress across her cheek, entrancing her even further. And still she drank in this gift of his approval, an approval she had never known.

'Is it a deal?'

'Deal?' she whispered huskily, her throat unaccountably dry and her tongue loath to work at all.

His gaze dropped to her mouth and she saw his own mouth make a sensual little movement as he drew closer. Her heart thumped an urgent warning, and her mind jagged alarm into life-suspended nerves, awakening them to danger. She heaved a sigh of exasperation at her idiotic vulnerability and stepped abruptly out of touch. She had to pull herself together, get out of the bedroom, get him out of the bedroom. Suddenly she was horribly, horribly conscious of his nakedness under that bathrobe.

'What did you have in mind?' she asked, swinging on her heel and marching back to the living-room, which was a far more sensible place for talking business. If he really meant to talk business.

The man was dangerous, a teasing, tantalising devil who was all too adept at leading his target up any number of garden paths. Confuse and conquer—it was a game to him, an amusing little game where he pressed the buttons and used the responses. But Lyn was not going to let herself be lured on to his sexual merry-go-round. She had purpose in her life now, and control, thanks to Aunt Henrietta. Peter Kelso could prod and tease as much as he liked, but he would not lead Lyn down any path without her taking a damned good look at the destination.

He followed her, completely at ease, giving no indication of frustration, simply carrying on the conversation as if it had never been diverted in any way. 'I think Sinclair would be the best man to approach. His showroom is the biggest, and the man has the style and taste to maximise the impact of any piece of art. And what's more, he'll be at the opening of Caswell's exhibition this evening.' The smile he gave Lyn was rich with satisfaction. 'Nothing like striking while the iron's hot. I shall enjoy drawing Charles into your lap.'

'Lap?' Her frown showed distaste for the word.

Peter grinned, disarming her once again. 'You don't know Charles Sinclair?'

'I don't think so.'

'We'll make him jump through hoops. He reminds me of a lapdog, exquisitely brushed up and turned out, and with the inbred skill to ingratiate himself to all customers. You must know his establishment, Interiors of Distinction?'

'Oh yes. My mother and sister dote on the place but ...' Lyn shrugged. 'I've never been there. I don't like shopping.' Not with them, she added silently.

Peter raised a quizzical eyebrow. 'Do you go to art galleries?'

She nodded. 'I read about Arnie Caswell having a new exhibition of sculptures. I don't usually go to openings, though. Too many people and too much chat for any serious viewing to be done.' And, of course, Delvene liked the social éclat of such events, and Delvene's presence invariably spoilt Lyn's enjoyment, one way or another.

'Today we have more important things to accomplish than viewing. I suggest we turn up at the exhibition at about seven. The formalities will be over by then and we can tackle Charles straight away.'

Lyn hesitated. Peter was sweeping her towards a course she was still not sure she wanted to take. But if he could swing a deal for her, it would settle any financial problems. And maybe the shop wasn't such a good idea. She would rather spend her time designing than attending to business. There could be no harm in trying the option he was holding out to her. 'All right,' she agreed slowly.

His smile held a hint of triumph. 'It'll be fun. Now, supposing I take you out to lunch to celebrate?'

'Thanks, but no, thanks,' she said firmly. She needed a breather away from Peter Kelso's dangerous attraction. 'I want to potter round and find places for everything here. And thanks again for all your help too. It really was very kind of you.'

He cocked a cheeky eyebrow at her. 'Is that a tactful dismissal?'

She sighed. 'Yes, it is,' she replied bluntly, all too aware that he could turn just about anything she said round the other way.

'Oh well, each to his own, but I still think my idea's better.' He strolled towards the door. 'Do you have an outfit of your own design? Something suitable for wearing to an exhibition?'

'Yes, I do.'

'I trust it's stunning?'

Her ... stunning? She could not repress a wry little smile. 'At least original and exclusive.'

'Wear it. Be ready to leave for Jessie's gallery at six-thirty.'

'Jessie?' The name tripped off Lyn's tongue with a slur of disbelief.

Peter's grin mocked her prurience. 'That vision of loveliness you saw me with earlier. You really should keep a more open mind, Lyn. Jessie's a very capable businesswoman.'

'As well as a very capable player,' she retorted with bite.

His grin grew wider, taking on a decidedly salacious look. 'Very capable. Want to try at equalling her?'

'Not today, thank you,' Lyn clipped out airily.

He gave her a wicked wink as he opened the door. 'Maybe tomorrow.'

She arched a sceptical eyebrow. 'I'll let you know when I'm free.'

'You do that. For you I'll make a point of being available.'

The door shut behind him before she could make a retort. She shook her head, wondering if she was crazy to get involved with him, even for a business deal. Mad, bad, and dangerous to know. The words slid into her mind and she recalled that they had been applied to the poet Lord Byron. They applied equally well to Peter Kelso, and Lyn's strong instinct for self-preservation advised keeping a safe distance.

But he had also been kind and helpful and genuinely interested in her work. Which was all very, very confusing. A shameless profligate and a good Samaritan. Some neighbour! she thought as she plunged into the business of settling in.

Lyn was sorting through her books when her mind suddenly connected the facts that Delvene would probably be at Arnie Caswell's opening and would see her with Peter Kelso. Instant scandal, as far as their mother was concerned. Anxiety cramped Lyn's heart for a moment until determination shrugged it off. What her mother thought and what her father thought had dominated her life for twenty-three years. That was quite long enough. She had made her decision and she would stick by it.

Peter Kelso's idea might be good and it might not. She would make her own judgement when the time came, but until then she would keep an open mind on the man. It was her life, her future. She had to put the past behind her and forge her own direction. She knew now that Aunt Henrietta had wanted her to do just that. And Peter Kelso had been Aunt Henrietta's confidant. That said he was worthy of some trust.

CHAPTER FOUR

As Lyn appraised her reflection in the mirror she knew she had never looked better. It was safe to wear the rose outfit now; Delvene could not get her beautiful, covetous hands on it. Lyn had cut the roses and leaves from an upholstering linen, shaping the appliqués round the neckline of the bodice. She had also used them to spray out from the nipped-in waist, hugging the hipline before trailing towards the hem of the full skirt. The coppery-red roses and leaves in their heavy linen sat beautifully on the dark green, crinkly cheesecloth, creating an effect which was both lush and dramatic, and the colours suited Lyn to perfection.

The rat-a-tat-tat on her apartment door was undoubtedly Peter Kelso's way of announcing himself. A glance at the bedside clock showed he was punctual. She quickly slid her feet into the green and copper sandals, picked up the matching handbag, and presented herself at the door.

The dark brown eyes gleamed approval. 'Perfect!'

Lyn smiled at Peter Kelso's echo of her own appraisal. 'Thank you,' she said with complete sincerity. She knew he was not lying, and his keen appreciation of her bedspread designs had convinced her that he had a very discriminating eye. His compliment was genuine and it made her feel

... perfect. 'Are those your wheeler-dealer clothes?'

He looked rich-sexy. A cream raw-silk jacket topped elegantly tailored trousers in a tan-bronze colour. His old-gold shirt was pure silk and specifically designed to a deep opening on his chest. Italian couture, Lyn decided, and she had no doubt that the chunky chain and gold medallion resting on his darkly tanned skin were the genuine article and not mere costume jewellery.

Peter grinned. 'Rules of the game. You dress to the taste of the target. When you're accepted as one of them, their guard is down, and you have the inside track.'

'Is everything a game to you, Peter?' she asked as they took the lift down to the garages.

His eyes twinkled sheer devilment. 'The fascination of life is in learning and mastering the rules. The satisfaction is in twisting them to your advantage. And winning makes it all worthwhile.'

He drove a Lamborghini—white, not red like most of the sports cars Lyn had seen, and custom-made, white lambswool seat covers, not the usual black upholstery. That extra touch of class for Peter Kelso, Lyn mused to herself. And he obviously liked the Italian touch.

She observed him slyly as they crossed the harbour bridge and headed for Domain Park. He had all the dash of a Mississippi gambler or a buccaneer, and the devious mind of the devil himself. She wasn't at all sure that any association with him could do her any good. But this was her gamble. And the die had been cast.

The art gallery was not one Lyn had frequented.

It dealt in fashionable artists rather than those trying to break new ground. The double-terrace house in Paddington had been elegantly restored, and even before one set foot inside the place it spelled out that anything for sale was going to cost big money. Arnie Caswell had made his name, and the people invited to his opening would only be people of wealth. Like Peter Kelso. And the Mansfields.

Jessie was in the foyer, graciously welcoming people and giving out a catalogue of the items on display. Her soignée appearance was in marked contrast to the rather dishevelled picture she had presented this morning. Sophistication muted her sexiness, and Lyn now realised that the woman was more Peter's age than her own. The lovely blue eyes lit with pleasure when they sighted Peter, but the pleasure dimmed somewhat as they slid to Lyn, and dimmed even more as they assessed Lyn's outfit. The smile on her mouth turned a little wry.

'Not wasting any time, Peter,' she said in a tone of dry amusement which did not quite veil a touch of chagrin.

Lyn flushed with embarrassment. She willed Peter to correct his girl-friend's misreading of the situation, but he didn't.

'Time is only wasted by people who don't know how to use it, Jessie. I'm not one of them,' he advised her good-humouredly.

The woman shrugged and offered a dry aside to Lyn. 'I hope you know where you're going, honey. No woman can pin this guy down. But I'm glad you've come, Peter. Charles thinks he has something for you. He's in his office.'

'Then this is his lucky day. I have something for Charles.' And with a jaunty little salute to Jessie, Peter led Lyn into the main salon.

'Have you no shame at all?' she muttered.

'None whatsoever.' He cast her a sly smile. 'But if your sensibilities are smarting, let me tell you that part of Jessie's motive for sleeping with me last night was to persuade me into coming here today. So that she could get a nice fat commission from Charles.'

'Charles Sinclair?'

'He owns the gallery. Jessie runs it.'

'Oh!' Oh indeed, Lyn echoed to herself. Being with Peter Kelso was certainly broadening her education. She supposed it did not really matter what Jessie believed. A woman of her dubious morals was unlikely to believe the truth anyway.

Peter steered her through a crowd of champagne-swilling patrons, not stopping to view Arnie Caswell's sculptures, then ushered her up a stair-case. As they reached the top landing he murmured, 'No matter what I say, don't interrupt the deal. Trust me. If you have to speak, follow my lead.'

Lyn nodded, relieved that he did not require much from her. Her stomach was turning queasy even as Peter knocked on the office door. She did not want to haggle over her art. It was terribly personal to her, part of her innermost soul. Before she had time to voice her second thoughts, Peter opened the door and pushed her inside. She flicked a nervous glance at the man standing behind the desk at the other end of the room and forgot all about her art.

He was beautiful—no other word for it. Classical

features moulded a fine, sensitive face. It was almost too perfect with its smooth, tanned skin and vividly blue eyes. Even the eyebrows were arched in perfect balance. The streaky blond hair was thick and held enough wave to enhance its fashionable cut. His physique looked perfect too. The blue and white pin-striped shirt and grey slacks carried no deceptive tailoring. Just looking at him quickened Lyn's pulse. He was, without a doubt, the most stunningly attractive man she had ever seen.

'Ah, Dorian. As handsome as ever,' Peter rolled out in his teasing lilt. 'Back from the fleshpots of Europe already?'

Lyn was only favoured with a cursory glance before the blue eyes projected boredom at Peter. 'I would be obliged if you could remember that my name is Damien.'

Peter snapped his fingers. 'Slip of the tongue. Somehow you always remind me of *The Portrait of Dorian Gray*—all veneer, no substance.'

Damien was not amused. 'Still envious, Peter?'

Peter's dry chuckle was mocking. 'I wouldn't take on your handicaps, Dorian ... I beg your pardon, Damien ... for all the money in the world.'

'Nor would I take on your ... defects,' Damien replied acidly.

'Well, that's settled,' declared Peter, grinning like the Cheshire Cat.

Settled! Lyn was aghast at the rancid antagonism he had stirred. She tried to think of something diplomatic to say when she was introduced, but Peter blithely denied her that courtesy.

'And now to business,' he burbled on. 'Where's your father? The good and faithful Jessie assured me he was waiting to be pleasured by my presence.'

'He'll be back in a moment.'

'Good! Take a chair, Lyn.' He pushed one up for her, then irreverently hitched himself on to the edge of the magnificent cedar desk. 'Damian tends to forget his manners when I'm around,' he added mischievously.

'Please do make yourself comfortable.' Damien said tightly, and irritation edged his voice as he added, 'Peter invariably does as a matter of course.'

Lyn sat down, but she was far from comfortable. Apparently Damien didn't care to seek an introduction to an associate of Peter Kelso, and Peter had no intention of giving one. Her stomach was getting queasier by the minute. She hoped that Peter enjoyed a more cordial acquaintanceship with the father or she couldn't see how any business could be done. Full of apprehension, she stole a covert glance at Damien. His gaze had been drawn to her rose outfit and a slight frown of puzzlement creased his forehead.

'Is this the merchandise Charles wanted to show me?' Peter enquired, lifting a small silver box from the desk and examining it closely.

Damien dragged his gaze away from Lyn's appliquéd dress and answered distractedly, 'Yes. A genuine Louis XIV snuffbox. I picked it up in France.'

'Taken to shoplifting now?' Peter tossed off casually, his attention still on the box. 'Girls too easy for you?'

Damien's jaw grew taut as if he was clenching his teeth. He made no reply, for which Lyn was thankful. Her nerves were already twanging from the hostile atmosphere in the room, and they leapt in apprehension as the door behind her opened. It gave her some relief to see Peter turn a beatific smile to the newcomer.

'There you are, Charles. I've come to do you a favour.'

'No, thanks very much,' came the swift, polite and firm retort. 'I've been on the receiving end of your favours before. They always cost me money.'

'Don't lie to me. You've always made money out of them. Not as much as you wanted to make, of course, but you made money.'

'A moot point. I see Damien has shown you the favour I'm offering you.'

He swept past Lyn with barely a flicked glance in acknowledgement of her presence. The carefully groomed abundance of white hair, flowing moustache and pale blue eyes might be suggestive of a lapdog to Peter, but to Lyn, Charles Sinclair looked formidable. His face was distinguished-handsome. His light grey suit was impeccably tailored. The pearl-grey tie looked exquisite on a pale pink shirt whose collar was held down by pearl studs. The hand which gestured towards the snuffbox was almost as beringed as Liberace's and his smile did not quite reach his sharp eyes. A shark in a dolphin suit was Lyn's immediate impression.

'I'm giving you first option on it. Beautiful, isn't it?' he said, his tone rich with persuasive appreciation.

Damien moved aside, looking only too willing to concede all sales talk to his father. He took a chair to the side of the desk and seemed to relax. Lyn wished she could too. Charles Sinclair had not looked for an introduction to her either, and again Peter did not offer one. The omission was very close to insulting and she did not understand it. The whole situation felt wrong to her.

'Mmh, very nice,' drawled Peter. 'But not unique. Lyn is. She makes bedspreads.'

The look Charles Sinclair gave her made Lyn feel like an unwanted insect. It was the kind of look she had often received from her parents and her instant reaction was to cringe inwardly. But that life was over, she reminded herself. She had no reason to cringe; her work was good. Her chin came up and her eyes returned a very cool dignity. It was Charles Sinclair who looked away.

'How nice for her!' The tossed comment was not the least bit interested. 'Notice the filigree work on the ...'

'And sells them,' Peter cut in carelessly.

The flicked look at Lyn was sharp and the mouth beneath the moustache set with resistance. 'That's harder,' he stated with bite.

'For five thousand dollars.'

Startled incredulity quickly settled into annoyance. 'Don't take me for a fool! There's no market at that price.' The face he turned to Lyn was a study of cold rejection. 'I'm sorry, miss, but I'm not going to waste your time or mine. No one will pay that sum for a bedspread. I'm simply not interested.'

Lyn said nothing. She was prickling with anger over his arrogant judgement. The man could at least have granted her the chance of showing her work! At this point she would have given up and walked out, but Peter made no move, and she had promised to follow his lead.

'You're quite right, Charles,' he said blithely. 'The price is now six thousand dollars—that's a sort of penalty for outright rejection. Van Gogh and Gauguin would understand. They had trouble with their dealers too.'

The pale blue eyes were diamond-hard. 'There's still no market.'

Peter smiled. 'There will be, Charles. When you see them.'

His silky provocation niggled. Charles gave up on the sale of the snuffbox, settled into the studded leather chair behind the desk and adopted a pose of haughty disdain. 'Really, Peter, I think you're slipping! Do you have to introduce your girl-friends to Charles Sinclair with the promise of some outrageous deal in order to extract a reward? A favour for a favour, so to speak?'

A wave of mortification brought spots of burning colour to Lyn's cheeks.

'I never confuse money and sex, Charles. One would alloy the pleasure of the other,' Peter stabbed at him before turning to Lyn and speaking in a tone of weary cynicism. 'Let this be a lesson to you, Lyn. Rejection without consideration, just because he thinks you're offering me the pleasures of your delightful femininity. Jealousy and envy. He'll certainly suggest a visit to his bed when he sees your work. Refuse it categorically. He's a dirty, sordid, lecherous man. A good sensible girl like yourself doesn't need his attentions to sell your work. Thank God Van Leeuwin prefers boys. He'll pay the price when he sees your work without any sexual bargaining at all.'

Lyn's mind was reeling with shock. Charles

Sinclair's snide crack had been bitter enough to swallow, but Peter's sexual lecture had been downright disgusting. She rose to her feet.

'This is intolerable!' Her voice trembled with outrage. 'I do not wish to deal with you, Mr Sinclair.' She turned bitterly accusing eyes up to Peter. 'Nor do I ever want to ...'

'Quite rightly so,' Peter cut in, hopping off the desk and squeezing her elbow hard. Without giving her time to complete her indictment of him, he switched his attention back to Charles, his voice whiplike in contempt. 'Until today, I respected your business acumen, Charles. Now I see you've degenerated to the level of your son.'

'This is libel!' Charles Sinclair grated out savagely.

'Tut-tut! You're losing your cool, Charles,' Peter reproved him mockingly. 'Besides, it's not libel, it's slander. You ruin my reputation by associating my sex life with money and I'll damned well ruin yours—your reputation, your sex life, and your financial position. I'm sorry, Charles. I've always enjoyed doing business with you, but I can't afford to be associated with you any more. And, of course, I shall have to comment on it in my newsletter.'

'That's blackmail!'

'No, dear boy. That's the price of stupidity.'

And on that line Peter turned Lyn away and began to escort her to the door. She could not get there fast enough, but Peter seemed intent on a slow, dignified withdrawal. She schooled herself to his pace, knowing that a few more moments would see the end of this scene. And the end of Peter Kelso as far as she was concerned. Some gamble she had tried! She had been off her brain even to think of trusting him.

'Oh, come now,' Charles Sinclair blustered behind them. 'There's been some little misunderstanding here . . .'

'There certainly has,' Peter agreed curtly, turning towards Charles as he put his hand on the doorknob. 'You've insulted the lady and her work, not to mention my integrity, and I bitterly resent it.'

Insulted! God, he ought to talk! Lyn fumed.

Charles Sinclair shot him a malevolent look. 'You have my apology. And I have no intention whatsoever of trying to seduce the young lady.'

Peter's hand slid off the doorknob. 'I should hope not. I want that pleasure to be all mine.'

Never, Lyn promised him with silent venom. Her hand reached for the doorknob, but Peter ambushed her intention, catching her hand and imprisoning it in his. She glared defiance at him.

Charles cleared his throat. 'Well, then. Perhaps we can reach some amicable arrangement. If the goods should prove marketable.'

Peter's eyes bored into hers, commanding that she should trust him. 'Lyn refused fifty thousand dollars for one of her creations this morning,' he said with a quirky little smile.

It was the smile that unsettled Lyn's defiance.

'Did you?' Charles Sinclair demanded of her, his voice sharp with incredulity.

'Yes,' Lyn tossed at him haughtily, too worked up to care what was said any more. Peter's eyes twinkled approval. Her shell-shocked mind slowly grasped that this was all a game to him and everything he said had a purpose. Even that crazy bid of fifty thousand dollars this morning. He was pushing psychological buttons and manipulating the reactions. Her gaze moved to the man behind the desk, wanting now to see if her theory was correct.

Charles Sinclair's frown mixed disbelief with a remote possibility that perhaps there was something for him in this deal. 'Sit down, sit down, we'll talk business,' he commanded abruptly. 'What price are you putting on that bedspread?' he shot at Lyn as Peter led her back to the chair.

'I already have first option,' Peter pounced in triumphantly. 'It's not for sale—to you, or to anyone else.'

Lyn sat down, absolutely staggered by her sudden insight of what was happening. Peter resumed his perch on the desk with the air of a man in complete control. And maybe he was, she mused. He had just forced Charles Sinclair to jump through one hoop.

Charles flicked him a look of sharp calculation. 'If this is as good as you say . . . yes, it does have possibilities.' He cast a patronising smile at Lyn. 'I'll look. I can't commit myself until then, but I'll look. Perhaps we could do a deal on consignment.'

Lyn could hardly believe her ears. He was going to deal. Peter had broken down his resistance. She shook her head in dazed wonderment and was further bemused when Peter used her hapless gesture.

'Lyn doesn't wish to deal on consignment. You pay for what you take,' he declared decisively.

'At five thousand dollars retail!' Charles sniped.

'Four thousand cost. Six thousand retail.' Peter smiled sweetly. 'Remember you looked a gift horse in the mouth and got a nasty kick in the teeth.'

Lyn only just stopped herself from rolling her eyes. It seemed to her that Peter was kicking a horse which had already been overworked.

Again came the frown. 'You really think her work's that good? I can sell it for that?'

'It's that good.'

Peter held Charles Sinclair's sceptical gaze with smug confidence. Finally Charles heaved a sigh of surrender. 'All right. Tomorrow at the showroom.'

'I'll bring the contract. I've seen you at work before, Charles, and we'll have no fine print. The bottom line is four thousand, but I have no doubt you'll raise the retail price on some of Lyn's work, if not all. I know you specialise in high mark-ups. So we'll write in that Lyn gets sixty per cent of any amount over the six thousand mark. I won't allow you to feather your bed with Lyn's talent.'

Charles grimaced at the double entendre and shot a pained look at Lyn. 'I assure you, miss . . .'

'Mansfield,' Peter supplied silkily. 'Miss Lynette Mansfield, the younger daughter of Gerald and Alicia Mansfield. I'm sure you know the name, Charles. It's been in the top echelon of Sydney society for a long, long time. I understand they're customers of yours.'

Shock gave way to a complete reconstruction of Charles Sinclair's manner. He came out of his chair like a ship in full sail, billowing round the desk with hands flapping appeasement. 'My dear Miss Mansfield! You see I am the victim of Peter's unkind entrapment. His eccentricities drive one beyond discretion. And indeed, you could have come directly to me . . .'

'And while he stroked you with one hand, he would have robbed you with the other,' Peter inserted sardonically.

'He does me a disservice. I'm a businessman, Miss Mansfield, and one must cover risks.' Charles Sinclair smiled indulgently. 'I'm sure you understand.'

'Yes, I understand,' Lyn said coldly, despising the man for his reaction to the Mansfield name. Peter had known his mark all right—a lapdog, with a nasty nip for those he considered beneath his notice. Only Peter had nipped back even harder. Such a hypocritical snob deserved to be discomfited, and Lyn no longer minded Peter's outrageous manipulation. He had won her a deal—a deal beyond her wildest dreams.

Peter smiled devilish delight at her as he unhitched himself from the desk and stepped over to lift her to her feet. Damien also came forward. He had remained silent throughout the highly charged dialogue, and Lyn had been too humiliated and embarrassed even to glance at him after his father had started the sexual insinuations. But now she met his gaze with steely pride.

'Miss Mansfield, if it's not too personal a question, may I ask if you designed your dress?'

The question was put with such charming interest that Lyn flushed with pleasure. 'Yes, it's my design. And the only one of its kind. Like my bedspreads,' she added with pointed emphasis.

Damien smiled at her, the blue eyes lighting with avid interest. 'Then I look forward to seeing you and your bedspreads tomorrow.'

Somehow Damien's admiration and approval

lent a more solid reality to the deal. He would see her tomorrow. And her bedspreads. Lyn's face relaxed into a responding smile.

'Yes, yes,' Charles Sinclair agreed quickly. 'Delighted to be doing business with you, Miss Mansfield.'

'Don't forget to thank me for the favour, Charles,' drawled Peter as he steered Lyn towards the door.

Charles opened it for them and pasted a smile on his face for Peter. 'One of these days your Machiavellian sense of humour will be your undoing, dear boy. I shall thank you for the favour tomorrow.'

The door was closed on Peter's laughter and he swept Lyn into an exuberant hug. 'Satisfied?'

He was undeniably mad. And shamelessly bad. But right at this moment Lyn couldn't take him to task for the dreadful things he had said. He had achieved for her what she could never have achieved for herself, and for that she was intensely grateful, no matter how much he had made her squirm.

'Yes, thank you,' she said graciously, then in wry comment, 'I've just died a thousand tortured deaths, but I am satisfied, thank you very much.'

He laughed and linked her arm with his. 'Relax— it's in the bag. Now we can really enjoy ourselves. A little stroll round the exhibition, just in case Arnie Caswell has come up with a brilliancy, and then a fine dinner at Luigi's to unwind completely. See how I look after you?'

Lyn rolled her eyes heavenwards. As Peter led her downstairs she began to giggle. It was very difficult to control her sense of hysteria. Only this morning she had left the Mansfield mansion and the whole refined, static way of life it represented. She had wanted to get her life moving, and moving it certainly was. With Peter Kelso the world turned upside down and inside out.

But being with him certainly carried penalties as well as prizes. Apart from her needing a very strong heart to withstand the shocks he handed out so blithely, Lyn's reputation was in danger of being shot to shreds. Jessie was in no doubt about Lyn's destination tonight, and God only knew what Damien and Charles Sinclair thought.

'Did you have to say you wanted to seduce me?' she asked wryly.

Peter arched a shocked eyebrow at her. 'Would you want me to tell a lie?'

'Not at all,' she answered airily. 'Blow the whole world to smithereens, but never, never lie.'

He grinned and tucked her arm possessively round his. 'Nice to be with a woman who shares my own sense of integrity.'

Integrity! The giggles erupted again and Lyn started to wonder if his madness was infectious.

Peter steered her round the exhibition, but she might as well have been a marionette for all she saw. Her mind was still coming to grips with what had taken place in the upstairs office. The more she thought about it, the more she appreciated just how much Peter had done for her. He was a manipulator of people and situations—no doubt about it. She felt a growing respect for the agility of his mind and his remarkably shrewd perception.

The deal he had struck for her was absolutely

fantastic, if it came off tomorrow. But there was no reason not to be confident. Peter was certainly confident or he would not have bargained like that. Lyn was just beginning to enjoy a relaxed optimism when Peter led her into yet another display room— and there was Delvene.

CHAPTER FIVE

SHE stood out like a brilliant ray of sunshine, Delvene the beautiful, her tall, traffic-stopping figure poured into a yellow-and-white silk dress which screamed couturier label, her silky blonde mane rippling with her laughter, her face full of perfect features set in gracious acceptance of the adoration projected at her from a coterie of admirers.

Lyn's eyes held no adoration. She stood there as mesmerised as a rabbit caught in floodlights while the old familiar panic screeched around her nerves. Delvene would spoil everything. She always did for Lyn. She would stir up trouble for her with their parents, and Lyn didn't want any more of that. Not when the future was looking so promising.

She tugged at Peter's arm in a bid to draw him away before he attracted Delvene's notice, and he raised enquiring eyebrows. Lyn was about to say she was terribly hungry when she saw the twitch of Delvene's private antenna which invariably alerted her whenever a personable male hit the perimeter of her vision. Questing green eyes zoomed in on Peter. They liked what they saw—there was no mistaking their acquisitive gleam.

Lyn shut her mouth on a resigned sigh. It was too late to escape. In a second or two Delvene would notice her and the fat would be in the fire. There was no other course but to brazen out the situation.

Her backbone stiffened. She had nothing to be ashamed of, no reason to run away and hide. She had done nothing wrong, and Peter Kelso had done her a lot of good.

The green gaze slid sideways for a quick measure of Peter's companion. Lyn put on a dismissive smile of hail and farewell, nursing a hopeless hope that just for once her sister would remain content with what she already had. Lyn could not enjoy the surprise on Delvene's face. The surprise would be even greater when Delvene learnt Peter's identity.

A sharp line of irritation appeared between Delvene's eyes as they evaluated Lyn's clothes, and vexation tightened her mouth for a moment before it curved into a patronising smile. The rose outfit had escaped her, but the man would not, Lyn interpreted. The Delvene Machine moved straight into action—a sweetly-mouthed excuse to the courtiers, followed by a gracefully confident approach.

Lyn could feel herself shrink. No matter that Delvene was peeved that the rose outfit had escaped her. In the final analysis clothes meant nothing. Delvene knew she could always win over her younger sister.

'Why, Nettie . . .' Trilled music which curdled Lyn's stomach. 'Fancy seeing you here! I thought you always snubbed these dos.'

Which translated as 'introduce me to your man'.

Lyn obliged. There was no point in refusing. Delvene was perfectly charming at introducing herself. 'Delvene, meet Peter Kelso. Peter, my sister Delvene.'

Shock widened the green eyes, but it was quickly

dispersed by Delvene's super-ego. Lyn could read her like a book—the pages were all too familiar. If her younger sister had attracted this man then Delvene would override the attraction. Lyn did not look up at Peter's face. While she had no claim on him, he had given her his time, used his agile and eccentric mind on her behalf, and made her feel rather special, valued. She could not bear to watch that value wink out as Delvene flexed her power.

'Well, well! Auntie's pet tiger.' Delvene batted her curly eyelashes flirtatiously. 'She really was very mean not to introduce you to me.'

'A criminal oversight. But then women can be such cats. Your aunt never did appreciate the physical ... as I do,' Peter purred suggestively.

Lyn almost gagged. Then she immediately derided herself. What other response could she have expected from Peter Kelso, the virtuoso of all physical games? Of course he would find Delvene's superb equipment worth testing.

Delvene tinkled laughter. 'I must say you were a curiosity to us, wasn't he, Nettie?'

Lyn gave the perfunctory smile to the perfunctory aside. Good manners were a habit. She wondered how Delvene would react if she flew at her tooth and nail. Lyn startled herself with the vehemence of that thought. Peter owed her no loyalty. He had delivered the deal he had promised. She certainly didn't want him to seduce her, but something deep inside her didn't want Delvene to share that intimacy with him either.

'I delight in satisfying curiosity,' Peter purred again. 'How astute you are to find my weakness at the first stroke!'

Delvene preened.

Lyn started to slide her hand out of Peter's hold. If he wanted Delvene he could have her, but Lyn didn't want to be associated with him any more. His fingers tightened round hers, denying her move to detach herself. She tugged in vain and gave up resentfully.

'Since Nettie is now your neighbour, we can really make your acquaintance,' Delvene invited.

Lyn gritted her teeth. Like hell they were going to use her apartment! It was her home!

'It would always be a pleasure to see you, Delly.'

Delly! Delly!!! Lyn went into shock. No one, literally no one had ever dreamed of corrupting Delvene's name in any way, let alone to Delly! The association of garlic sausages and aromatic cheeses was so marvellously incongruous that Lyn was hard put not to explode with hysterical laughter.

It was too much for Delvene. Her smile looked like cracking. She just had to correct him. 'I am always called Delvene, Peter.' And there was a perceptible cooling of her manner as she stood on her dignity.

Most men would have rushed to appease the offence, but not Peter Kelso. He burbled on in grand style. 'But as a close connection of the family you must allow me a little indulgence. As long as Lyn remains Nettie to you, you will have to remain Delly to me. I do so like these childish games.'

A glorious bubble of joy blossomed inside Lyn. Peter was taking her side against her sister, her very beautiful sister! No man had ever done that before. Her fingers squeezed his in an excess of happiness.

He squeezed back. Lyn could hardly contain her delight.

A look of puzzled disbelief was discomposing Delvene's golden glow of assurance. She was not accustomed to having her wishes disregarded. 'I don't like it, Peter,' she informed him with pointed emphasis.

'But I like it, Delly. And I like you. You're so very beautiful, so wonderfully composed, so ravishingly innocent. Yes, innocence expresses it perfectly. But for the moment I'm under Lyn's spell. If she should tire of me, discard me like a dirty dishrag, then I'll come to you and worship at the altar of your beauty. Not from too great a distance, of course. I believe I would enjoy teaching you how to please me, and our lovemaking would surely drive you beyond anything you've ever known. But it's up to Lyn. For the present I must stay with your sister.'

Delvene was stupefied. Her mouth opened and closed and opened again, without any sound being emitted. Delvene the beautiful, the poised, the adored, the one who could do no wrong, was floundering like a fish out of water.

But Lyn herself was caught between elation that Peter had stood up for her and horror at the way he had done it. Delvene was sure to report it all to her parents and there would be no escaping an uproar. No one was going to believe that Lyn's only business with Peter Kelso was business. Prizes and penalties, she thought again in dry irony.

Peter let go her hand and curved a possessive arm round her shoulders, reinforcing his declaration of devotion. 'Please excuse us, Delly, but we were just on our way to dinner. Lyn has an appetite to match my own.'

But Delvene was puffed up to say something and she could not accept being brushed aside. Not by a man. Particularly not by a man who was favouring her younger sister with his attention. She clutched Lyn's free arm in a vicelike grip as Peter began to draw her away. 'He's going to ruin your reputation, Nettie!' she hissed, attacking her sister directly.

Peter's support and an even stronger sense of self-determination voiced a reply. 'I'd rather you call me Lyn, Delvene.'

'Lyn, Lyn, Lyn!' Delvene muttered irritably. 'Your being seen with him is bound to cause talk. As for your having an affair with him, Mummy will be furious!'

Lyn eyed her sister's heightened colour from a curious kind of distance. She had never seen a seriously thwarted Delvene before, and somehow her sister no longer seemed so all-conquering in her beauty. 'I'm not living in Mummy's pocket any more, Delvene,' she answered calmly, and her self-confidence grew as her sister shrank back.

'No, you're obviously living in someone else's!' The spite was off her tongue before she could catch it back, but she quickly recomposed her air of virtue. 'Nettie! What's got into you? Can't you see . . .?'

'Yes, I can see all right, Delvene, and I really don't need your advice, so why don't you go back to your boyfriends?'

Peter chuckled and cast a doting look at Lyn. 'Ah, she's magnificent, isn't she, Delly? Such strength of character. I can't wait any longer. I must carry her away.'

He swept Lyn off while Delvene was still swallowing. Lyn's previous sense of hysteria caught up with her again and she was giggling uncontrollably by the time they had made their exit complete. She was ruined in the eyes of her family, absolutely ruined. And here she was hanging on to the man who had ruined her.

But the marvellous reality was that she didn't care. She felt free, free of Delvene's shadow for the first time in her life. She loved the stern old aunt who had given her the push she had needed, and almost loved the outrageous man at her side who had fulfilled his promises. Except that he was mad and bad and terribly dangerous to any peace of mind. But right now she didn't even care about that.

'Lead on, Macduff,' she cried recklessly, riding a high which was too good to question.

Peter slanted her a mischievous look. 'I believe the quotation is, "Lay on, Macduff, and damned be him who first cries, hold, enough." Are you challenging me?'

Lyn laughed and shook her head. His knowledge did not surprise her. She didn't think anything about Peter would surprise her any more. 'I'm damned already,' she told him gaily.

'Not in my eyes,' Peter said with a warm smile of approval.

And for some crazy reason his approval more than balanced the disapproval her family would shower on her for being with him.

CHAPTER SIX

DINNER at Luigi's was fun. Peter's conversation could never be labelled dull, and Lyn's inner exhilaration bubbled out as freely as the champagne they drank with the meal. She would have been quite happy to bubble on all night, but Peter called a halt.

'We have an early start tomorrow,' he declared, adopting an air of responsibility.

'You think we should go to the showroom early?'

'Definitely not. First off we go to my printer and get some fancy name cards done, to sit on your bedspreads. Class publicity. What printing do you favour?'

'Nothing but copperplate.'

'In gold.'

'Gold and black.'

'You're the artist.'

Lyn laughed, feeling a surge of excitement at the thought of success.

'I'll make a two o'clock appointment with Charles. It's bad form to look too eager, and my solicitor will need the time to draw up your contract.'

It suddenly struck Lyn just how much Peter was doing for her. 'You're being very generous, Peter. I feel rather guilty for taking up so much of your time,' she told him.

He grinned. 'I have no better use for it.'

She eyed him curiously. 'What about making your own living? You must do some work since you put out a newsletter.'

He waved a careless hand. 'A mere sideline. It amuses me to keep the sharks honest. Ever heard of Joseph L Livermore, Lyn?'

'No.'

The brown eyes glittered with an inner excitement as Peter enlightened her. 'He was the great bear of Wall Street. He would sit and wait, only hitting the market once in every few years. When he did he backed his judgement against the greatest financiers of his time. And he won, Lyn, every time, using his own judgement and nerves of steel. But before he gambled he made sure that all the odds were on his side. If there's one particular person I admire, it's Joseph L Livermore.' He smiled, and it was the smile of a man who had known similar success. 'And in between raids you rest so that you don't overstrain your heart.'

He was indeed a gambler and he loved it. And he won, just as he had won for her tonight. 'So that's why your name is always headlines in the newspapers. When you win, you win big.'

His eyes glinted again with that inner relish as he stood up to help her out of her chair. 'I do enjoy the challenge. It's not really gambling, Lyn. It's brains and knowledge and technique. But in the meantime we're doing Charles Sinclair a favour.'

A favour. Lyn smiled at the absurdity and could not help smiling all the way home, but the smile received a jolt as they took the lift up to their apartment floor.

'It's time for you to repay your debts,' Peter murmured suggestively.

The shock to Lyn's heart was severe. He couldn't mean ... no, surely not. He had been so definite. No strings attached, no sexual bargaining. She couldn't believe he had lied about that. Not Peter Kelso. He would scorn such a ruse.

Her sharp glance found that a quirky smile was on his lips, a teasing twinkle in his eyes. She relaxed again. Peter was only playing. She was beginning to recognise the quirkiness of his mind. 'What do you want, Peter? The bedspread?' And although she was loath to let it go, he had done so much for her tonight that she was prepared to give it up.

He leaned back against the side wall, folded his arms and slanted his eyebrows in mock consideration. 'I think you owe me a cup of coffee.'

She smiled at the simplicity of the request, but her smile quickly faded into a sigh. 'I owe you far more than that. I could never, never have done it myself. You were terribly clever. If I can ever repay you ...'

'You owe me nothing, Lyn. Nothing at all. Except a cup of coffee.' He chuckled, his whole face alight with mischievous humour. 'I've had my reward for services rendered—the pleasure of seeing the expressions on Charles Sinclair's face. The pleasure of seeing you happy. The pleasure of helping to set you free.'

His smile curled round her heart, lifting it into a joyous beat. 'It's been a grand night,' she breathed on a sigh of sheer happiness. A grand night. The grandest night of her life. The lift doors opened, and as they moved to step out on to their floor Lyn impulsively took Peter's hand and squeezed it with emotion-laden fingers. 'Thank you for making it happen.'

He glanced down at her, saw the deep well of gratitude in the large, expressive eyes and rejected it. 'Hey, don't go serious on me! Life isn't that intense. It's meant to be fun, to be enjoyed to the full, to be free.'

Exhilaration came zinging back. 'We've sure done that!' she agreed as she unlocked her apartment door and flung it wide in welcome. 'Do you know how I feel? Like Eliza Doolittle when she got her speech right!' And hugging herself with happiness, Lyn waltzed round her living-room, giving triumphant voice to 'I Could Have Danced All Night'.

Peter closed the door and joined in, turning the dance into a mad romp until Lyn collapsed with laughter. 'Enough! You're too much, Peter,' she gasped, dropping into the nearest chair, then breaking into another peal of laughter. 'Oh God! Delly! How could you call my sister that? I thought her face would crack. I almost cracked up myself!'

Peter took off his jacket, dropped it on to the adjacent chair and propped himself against the armrest. He shook his head in grave consideration. 'Poor girl. You should feel sorry for her. She needs an awful lot of sorting out.'

'Delvene?' Lyn looked her incredulity. 'But she's got everything.'

One eyebrow shot up in arched mockery. 'Does a sunflower compare with a rose? All that golden glitter is mere tinsel.'

She laughed at him, caught up in his madness,

and loving it. She sprang up and hopped on to the coffee table, striking a triumphant pose. 'Do you know what it's like to have climbed Mount Everes and looked down upon the whole world?'

His eyes twinkled his knowledge of her exhilara tion, sharing it, firing it into something more 'Absolutely. But tomorrow there's always anothe mountain to climb. The trick is to find a way roun it if you can't go over it.'

'But you always go over yours, don't you?'

A throaty chuckle accompanied his step toward: her. 'I try, Lyn. I always try,' he said as he lifted he down, and while his hands held her only very lightly, his eyes held her in a far more purposefu fashion, inviting, promising, desiring.

Lyn's heart thumped a wild tattoo of warning .. or was it excitement? Her mind jammed on conflicting array of messages. Her hands flutterec nervously from his shoulders to his chest, yet she could not bring herself to push away from him Truth forced the recognition that she did not wan to. She wanted him to kiss her, wanted to know the feeling of his mouth on hers, his arms round her holding her to the whole strength of him, cementing the sense of togetherness which had been their: tonight.

He watched the desire kindle and take hold. Ther slowly, very slowly, waiting for the inviting tilt of her head, his mouth came down to take what she was offering. Not greedily, almost reverently—soft whispering kisses, tantalising, sensual, provoking a quivering intoxication for more. Driven by the instinctive need to prolong the excitement, Lyn slic her hands up round his neck, keeping his head pressed down to hers.

Peter did not rush to take advantage of her encouragement. In fact, he let go his light grasp on her waist. One hand curled round the nape of her neck, fingers and thumb finding spots of extraordinary sensitivity and softly stroking. His other hand trailed up and down the curve of her spine, making her skin shiver with pleasure. Then it found another erotic line, from the soft underflesh of her upstretched arm to the swelling edge of her breast. And Lyn's shivery pleasure grew so intense that it was an emotional release to open her mouth to the gentle probe of his.

The delicate touch of this new intimacy aroused nuances of feeling which were unbelievably exquisite. And Peter's hands continued to find places to caress, employing a fragile feathering which gradually built into a refined torture. Lyn's body was trembling with the need for harder pressure when he finally gathered her in. Hard, imprinting his own arousal on her, freeing her mouth as she gasped from the melting weakness that shot through her, then taking it again in a passionate plunder which fired a wildly abandoned response.

A primitive fever was in her blood and her soft flesh exulted against the aggressive muscularity of his. She wanted more of him. More. More. Her own hands were clutching, kneading, clawing, as possessive as the hands which were moulding her contours to his, curving round her bottom and ...

Oh God! No! The agonised cry pierced the intoxicated haze which had blanked out her mind. The image of Peter's clinch with Jessie shot into it with paralysing clarity. Her hands stopped their mad scrabbling. Her body froze into cramped pain and her mouth lost its passion.

Peter reacted on the instant of change, softening his embrace, hands turning back to seductive persuasion, lips brushing her ear. 'Don't stop now Lyn. Don't deny yourself,' he murmured huskily 'You have an ache, a pain, a need that must be fulfilled. Don't stifle it. Be free. Fly with me. Let me teach you what it is to be loved.'

She shuddered under his touch. But it was not from pleasure. 'It's not love, Peter,' she said flatly and sucked in a steadying breath. He was right: she did feel an ache, a terrible empty pain, but she knew her needs could not be fulfilled on a purely physical plane. She pulled back from him enough to challenge his desire. 'How many times a day do you want it?'

The dark eyes glittered down at her, burning into her soul, charring the edges of her resolve. 'With you I'd try for a record. But it's not only for me, Lyn. It's for you. I'd do everything I could to please you.'

He was the pied piper of sex and her pulse raced to his tune, but she shook her head, asserting her own will. 'I'm sorry, Peter. It's a bit like the bedspread. I'm not available, either for a price or as a gift.'

His mouth made that sensual little movement which was almost hypnotic. 'Another hill to climb?'

'Your hill. Not mine.'

He smiled a slow, provocative smile and took her wrist in his hand. He held it hard and she looked up at him in puzzlement. His eyes held hers, hotly purposeful in a strange, still silence. Then softly, suggestively, he spoke. 'Feel your own pulse, Lyn. It's doing two hundred and twenty beats to the minute. Keep that up any length of time and you're a dead woman. Come to bed with me and I'll save your life.'

She sighed as a smile tugged at her own mouth. 'I can't help my responses. You can do things to me physically, Peter, and no doubt you're a great lover. But the answer is still no.' She broke away and quickly headed for the kitchen, escaping from any further temptation. 'I'll make that coffee I owe you.'

He trailed after her. 'Think of what you owe yourself.'

'That's precisely what I am thinking of,' she retorted emphatically. 'I almost lost myself trying to fit in with what others wanted or expected of me. I'm finished with doing things I don't really want to do.'

She turned her back on his quizzical look and switched on the coffee-maker, desperately trying to fight off the lingering after-effects of fever-pitch arousal. She heard Peter settle himself on the kitchen stool. She could feel his eyes boring into her.

'So why are you refusing what you do really want?' There was no banter in his voice, nor any hint of persuasion. His tone was completely serious.

Lyn shook her head and slowly turned to face him, her eyes reflecting the bleak emptiness in her soul. 'It's not what I want, Peter. All my life I've been given lip-service love. Never the substance. And that's all you would give me tonight ... lip-service love. It might be physically exciting and pleasurable, but the pleasure would pass, and afterwards I would feel more lonely than ever for having given so much of myself away.'

He slid off the stool and took the couple of steps which separated them. Lyn tensed, determined to reject any physical overture he might make. He gently cupped her face in his hands, forcing her to look into eyes which held a strange, compelling glitter.

'Did you feel lonely with me tonight, Lyn?'

'No,' she whispered, fighting the tug of his personal magnetism.

'Nor did I feel lonely with you. We were together, Lyn. Why not share a closer togetherness?'

She summoned up a mocking smile. 'Like you had with Jessie last night? And who would it be tomorrow night? I'd just be another bit of exercise for you, sandwiched in between innumerable Jessies.'

He did not return her smile. His eyes seem to darken, and Lyn's skin prickled under the intensity of his gaze. 'I've never gone to bed with a woman I didn't like, Lyn. Nor have I ever gone to bed with a woman who didn't want to be there with me. I make no apologies for the Jessies in my life, nor do I apologise for enjoying sex, or any of the other things I do. But all of them would be considerably enhanced if I had the right partner with me. I've been searching for a long time, but I haven't found her. Yet.'

The emphasis he gave the last word squeezed her heart. Was Peter suggesting that she might be the right partner for him? Or holding out the possibility as an inducement to play his games? 'Trying out sex partners might be your way, Peter, but it's not mine,' she replied forcefully. 'I made up my mind yesterday that I wasn't going to live my life on anyone's terms but my own.'

'And you won't take a gamble?'

She could feel his will fighting hers. It was extremely difficult to repel the seductive power he was exerting, but Lyn clung to her resolve. 'I've done enough gambling for today,' she asserted firmly.

To her surprise his mouth curved into a whimsical smile and his hands left her face with a tender caress. 'Then I'll wait. For you I'll always be available, but I won't ask you again. When you feel ready you can tell me. Meanwhile the coffee is bubbling.'

In some considerable confusion of mind Lyn turned away from him and went about the business of filling their mugs automatically. 'Let's take it out on to the balcony,' she suggested, feeling the need for cool air on her fevered brow.

Peter relieved her of his mug, his darkly knowing eyes teasing her as he did so. 'Old Henry preferred the darkness of the balcony too. For speaking thoughts she found uncomfortable in the light of day.'

'I'm not Old Henry,' Lyn retorted emphatically.

'No, but you're like her. One day you'll see yourself as I see you, then you'll know how special you are.'

The words tugged at her heart, making it thump uncomfortably. She heaved a sigh to ease her constricted chest and led the way out. It was a beautiful night. The lights of the city were matched by the stars in a crystal-clear sky. The balcony held two sun-loungers and a table. Lyn was glad to sink on to one of the loungers, in the semi-darkness. She was badly shaken in body and mind.

She glanced surreptitiously at Peter as he stretched out on the other lounger. He was a very masculine man, attractive, virile, undoubtedly experienced in every erotic technique ever learnt. And very, very clever. And what was she? An ugly duckling with a talent for design. No match for Peter Kelso. Not like Delvene. The old sense of inferiority wormed around her mind.

'Why did you take my side against Delvene, Peter? She's very beautiful,' Lyn prompted warily.

'But with a very greedy heart. All Delvene has *is* her beauty and she knows it, which is why she wields it all the time to reassure herself that it's enough. You have so much more, Lyn.'

It seemed an extraordinary statement, yet Lyn felt gratified by it. Until she remembered Peter's words to Delvene. 'You said you'd make love to her,' she reminded him pointedly.

'Only if you toss me aside.' His grin flashed white in the darkness. 'And you're not going to toss me aside, are you?'

'Not as a friend, no,' she answered with absolute certainty. Lyn was beginning to understand Aunt Henrietta's friendship with him. There would have been an attraction of minds between them. 'A genius and a fool.' The words echoed through Lyn's thoughts, taking on many nuances of meaning. 'Why do you risk your life doing dangerous things like sky-diving?' she asked curiously.

'Because I've always wanted to experience everything life has to offer. If I died tonight, I wouldn't be dying with any regrets that I'd left undone what I wanted to do.'

'You've done your utmost to do it all.'

'And why not? You only live once. Open your mind, Lyn. Don't be shackled by fear.'

Fear? Yes, she had been shackled by fear, the fear of being rejected. But that fear was well grounded. Rejected by her parents. Rejected by men whose interest in her had waned when they had met Delvene. But not rejected by Peter. And she hadn't been rejected by Charles Sinclair either, thanks to Peter. It was she who had done the rejecting tonight. And she wasn't going to be shackled by fear any more. She glanced appreciatively at the man who was still here at her side, giving her his friendship even though she had refused him her body.

'It's not that I'm afraid of sex, Peter,' she said impulsively.

He cocked an eyebrow at her. 'Is that a subtle way of asking me to go to bed with you?'

She smiled and shook her head. 'When you can give me your soul, that's when I'll ask.'

He did not smile. He regarded her seriously for an uncomfortable length of time before he spoke. 'I'm my own man, Lyn, just as you want to be your own woman. I don't think you'll find that souls give much satisfaction.'

'Maybe they will one day. Anyway, that's my hill to climb,' she insisted sadly.

'Some hills are of your own making, Lyn.' His mouth curved into a provocative grin. 'But I'll be waiting for you when you come back down.'

He probably would be too, she thought with an odd sense of inevitability. But that was one descent she had to avoid. She wanted love, and Peter would only ever offer her sex.

He put his empty coffee mug on the table and swung his legs off the lounger. 'Well, I guess I'd better take myself off to my lonely bed and leave you to yours. Which seems a very wasteful arrangement. However . . .' He rose to his feet and drew Lyn to hers, eyes twinkling provocatively. 'The time will come.'

She could not resist challenging his confidence. 'Please don't hold your breath.'

He laughed and kept hold of one of her hands as he walked towards the front door, picking up his jacket on the way. The idle caress of his fingers reminded her all too sharply of the physical magic of which he was a master. Was she a fool to have turned him down? She wondered, then swiftly rejected the idea. She was not going to be a sexual exercise companion for anyone. But she did owe Peter far more than a cup of coffee.

'I'll make you a bedspread as a thank-you gift,' she promised as he opened the door.

He paused and looked down at her, a little smile of bemusement on his lips, a disturbing warmth in his eyes. 'Don't do that, Lyn. The only bedspread I want is yours, and the only way I want it is with you under it. With me. Just tell me when you want that too.' He touched a light finger to her lips. 'Sweet dreams.'

The door was closed quietly after him, and then it was Lyn who stood there in bemusement. She knew it would be wrong for her, she knew she would hate herself for it afterwards. But she could not help wishing that it could be all right. She wanted to know, to feel what it was like to have Peter Kelso as her lover.

But she made no move to go after him. Instead she went to her own lonely bed, lay under her bedspread by herself, and found some consolation in the thought that it was the more sensible and lasting relationship to have him as a friend.

Like Aunt Henrietta. The thought was disturbing. Here she was in her aunt's home, in her bed, and while she was not yet an old maid she was still a maiden in the sexual sense of the word. Any romance that might have developed into something more intimate had always been nipped in the bud by Delvene.

Lyn's mind quickly argued that she was only twenty-three. Surely in the years ahead she would find someone she could love, and who would love her. She did not want to go through life unloved, alone, not even having known the physical pleasure of lovemaking. But Peter Kelso's offer was the last resort. Definitely the last resort, Lyn told herself sternly as she drifted towards sleep.

But for some niggling reason the words 'good sensible girl' mocked her from a series of formless dreams.

CHAPTER SEVEN

THEY arrived on the dot of two. Peter directed the man in the loading bay office to carry in the bedspreads from the car.

'We could have carried them in ourselves,' Lyn muttered.

'Never take the chance of getting a bad back,' was the blithe answer.

She threw him a mocking look, but his face was pure innocence. Her sigh released a little of her pent-up feeling. She clutched her portfolio with tight, nervous fingers, a black leather portfolio, embossed with gold and carrying the signature 'Lyn Mansfield' in golden copperplate, acquired this morning on Peter's insistence. Along with the name cards and the contract from his solicitor and the black suit in French crêpe and the rich, creamy, frivolous blouse and the high, high heels.

Peter smiled down at her as he took her arm. 'I should always choose your clothes for you. I do a good job.'

Lyn looked up at him ruefully. 'I don't feel very me.'

'Then let's forget about selling bedspreads. I've got a better idea. We'll go home and slowly take off every garment. One by one. To make you feel more you, so to speak.'

Her traitorous mind slipped back to last night, recalling all too vividly the exquisite sensuality of his touch, the unbelievable excitement he had aroused without even attempting to remove any part of her clothing. The thought of those same hands peeling off each garment, slowly exploring her body, tantalising her with the erotic knowledge at his fingertips, driving her to an unbearable pitch of frenzied desire ... she shivered and sternly banished the fantasy. The frown she turned to Peter was a mixture of reproof and irritation over her own weakness. 'Don't you ever give up?'

His eyes danced with wicked mischief. 'Not when the object is desirable.'

Lyn shook her head. Incorrigible. And too damnably attractive for her to ignore completely the temptation he offered. 'I think we'd better concentrate on bedspreads,' she muttered.

He shrugged good-humouredly. 'Well, since you're ready for that, we shall proceed.'

'Interiors of Distinction' certainly lived up to its name, Lyn decided as Peter led her through the main showroom. All the furniture was quality and arranged with accessories of quality which showed it off to the best advantage. Peter steered her to the bedroom settings, relieved the man of the two bedspreads he had brought in and directed him to bring the third.

'Now which bed for which, Lyn?'

She looked her surprise at him. 'Shouldn't we wait for ...?'

'Not at all. Pretend we own the place,' he declared with the confident panache that was always his. 'Anyway, he's coming—unfortunately. I hoped we could do this together.'

Lyn looked in the direction of Peter's nod and

saw Charles Sinclair descending the stairs from a
mezzanine floor which overlooked the showroom.
A windowed office was set to the left of the staircase
and Damien Sinclair stood behind the glass,
watching her and Peter. Lyn felt a stab of
disappointment that he should choose to remain at
a distance.

I'll show him, she thought on an uncharacteristic
wave of confidence, and followed Peter's lead,
pointing out which bedroom settings would best
suit the designs she had made. As if she owned the
place. Peter was already rolling off one of the
bedspreads in preparation for laying out hers when
Charles arrived on the scene.

'Afternoon, Charles,' he said breezily. 'Where
would you like this dumped?'

'On the chair will do, thank you, Peter,' came the
frosty answer. He turned a smile full of polite charm
on to Lyn. 'Good afternoon, Miss Mansfield. I've
been looking forward to this moment all day.'

'That's very charming of you, Mr Sinclair. I hope
your sense of anticipation will be satisfied,' Lyn
replied, bubbling with inner happiness. She really
did feel confident.

The carrier returned with the third bedspread.
Peter thanked him and ushered him away. He took
the first from its plastic bag, and acting like a high
priest he reverently laid it out on the uncovered bed.
It was her Aztec design, shimmering gold raised
above brilliant vermilion on a rich velvet background of burnt sienna, edged with a pattern of
dark red.

Charles stared at it, enthralled by the interplay of
colour and fabric. His hand went out to touch, to

stroke. His head gave a little shake, just as Peter's had the day before. Lyn looked at Peter. His eyes danced triumph back at her. Her gaze lifted to the office window where Damien had stood. He was no longer there—he was descending the stairs in some haste.

'I hate to say I told you so, Charles,' Peter drawled provocatively.

To Lyn's surprise, Charles Sinclair chuckled. 'You have my gratitude. For this favour,' he added with dry emphasis, then turned to Lyn with a beaming smile. 'May I congratulate you, Miss Mansfield? I have seen many art works in my lifetime, but few of such stunning impact. I can say, with confidence, that Peter has not overvalued your extraordinary creativity.'

'Handsomely said, Charles,' Peter chimed in.

Lyn had no time to reply. Damien clapped his father on the shoulder, demanding his attention.

'You're taking it, of course,' was his insistent command.

'Of course,' Charles repeated blandly.

Damien's vivid blue eyes still gleamed with a devouring need to own as they fastened on Lyn. His smile was as dazzling as his eyes.

'A very great pleasure to meet you again, Miss Mansfield.'

His voice had a devouring quality too, and Lyn felt quite swamped as he took her hand in his.

'I take it you're impressed, Damien,' Peter remarked sardonically.

'More than impressed. Staggered!' The words were directed warmly at Lyn before Damien turned his head. 'Hello, Peter. Still gambling?' The antagonism was muted today, but the chilled bite to the words gave it away.

Peter smiled, amused by the sly dig. 'Only on certainties, Damien. As you can see for yourself. Ready for more?'

The two remaining bedspreads were laid out. Both the Sinclair men stood back, their arms folded, silently drinking in what they saw with avid eyes. Lyn did her best to hide her elation, but her eyes sparkled at Peter as he popped the name cards they had had printed below the centre of each bedhead.

'And now the signing of the contract, eh, Charles?' he suggested pointedly. 'I have it with me, all prepared for your signature. Perhaps you would like to peruse it. Though I assure you, it's not like yours. All above-board.'

Lyn almost swallowed her tongue as she smothered a gasp. She was aghast that Peter should choose to needle Charles now. It was unnecessary. It might even antagonise him into changing his mind at the last moment.

'And there's a small matter of a cheque for these three new acquisitions,' he burbled on. 'Oh, and Lyn has a portfolio of designs, if you'd care to place an order. Ten per cent deposit, naturally. If you choose any.'

But Peter knew his mark. Lyn noted with relief that Charles Sinclair was under his spell. Or hers.

'Naturally,' he echoed, and slowly dragged his gaze from the third bedspread to look at his son. 'The Italian shipment?'

Damien nodded and moved to take Lyn's arm, smiling his devastating smile. 'I have photographs of our incoming stock. If you'll come up to the office with me I'll show them to you, and you can show me your designs. Perhaps we can match the new bedheads to your work, to the enhancement of both.'

'And to our mutual satisfaction,' she responded warmly, feeling beautifully bubbly inside. Success was grand. Even grander if it meant dealing with a man as attractive as Damien Sinclair.

Peter and Charles followed them upstairs, casually discussing business takeovers and the rise and fall of the stock market. Lyn was so full of her own happiness that she didn't really listen, although she was amused to hear Peter say in his own inimitable way, 'Now, now, Charles, for that kind of information you need to pay big money. You shouldn't be imposing on my good nature like this.'

Damien bent his head close to Lyn's. 'They have no soul. I've travelled the length and breadth of Europe and not seen the like of your work.'

Lyn's heart gave a delighted skip. Her smile was even warmer when he opened the office door and ushered her inside. Two executive desks and a bank of files were set along the two closed-in walls. Armchairs and a coffee table were grouped along the glass sections. Damien went straight to a file drawer and withdrew a manila folder.

'We'll use my desk,' he suggested.

'Your coat, Lyn?' Peter murmured behind her, sliding the portfolio out from under her arm.

She threw him a grateful look. He was right, as always. It would be awkward stretching out her arms in the figure-hugging jacket. But before her hands even lifted to undo the buttons, Peter's deft fingers were at work, brushing against the swell of her breasts as they lightly pushed open each fastening. Too startled to stop him, she stared dumbstruck into knowingly provocative eyes. A warm surge of blood raced round her veins and her skin prickled with excitement.

For one awful moment she actually wanted him to touch her, wanted to feel his hands close over her breasts, and her nipples hardened into telling prominence. She was horribly aware of their arousal as Peter eased the jacket off her shoulders. Neither the frills nor the pintucks on the frivolous blouse were strategically placed to hide the fact.

She darted an agitated glance at the two Sinclair men, hoping that they would not notice her reaction to Peter's mischievous little intimacy. She found their eyes traversing the upthrust of her braless breasts, all too clearly delineated under the sheer material, although decently covered by a silk camisole. Embarrassment spurted heat into her cheeks, yet for all her embarrassment she was conscious of a secret, wholly feminine thrill.

It was not something she had ever looked for, but she experienced a flash of understanding for Delvene's fascination with sexual power. Knowing the men's eyes were following her, she walked with conscious grace, and a slight swing of the bottom, to the chair which Damien was holding for her. As she sat down the front split-pleat of her tight skirt stretched open. She caught Damien's appreciative glance at her darkly stockinged thighs before he sprang to business, laying the photographs out before her.

Lovely legs, Peter had declared. She smiled to herself, a pleasantly smug little smile which lingered on her lips as he placed the portfolio in front of her. She glanced up and he gave her a cheeky wink which almost tickled her into a silly giggle. She had no doubt that he had deliberately set out to make her feel sexy, but now she did not care. She felt great. Her work was appreciated and in demand. She was being treated with respect and looked at with admiration. Her cup was running over.

While she and Damien were making decisons about designs, Charles checked over the contract with Peter, discussing it in minute detail before attaching his signature. Peter added his as a witness and passed it to Lyn to sign, before writing his name again underneath hers.

Charles agreed to the ordering of three more bedspreads and wrote Lyn a cheque. Thirteen thousand and two hundred dollars. Not negotiable. Lyn stared at the figure with secret glee, then, with a feeling of immense satisfaction she tucked it away in her handbag.

Damien claimed her attention again, speaking with flattering eagerness. 'I have another proposition for you.'

'I told you this would happen, Lyn. Absolutely knew it! If it's not the father, it's the son,' Peter declared with sardonic humour.

'I'm serious,' grated Damien.

'Of course you are, who wouldn't be with such a find?' Peter retorted blithely. 'I am, too.'

Damien ignored him and turned eloquently pleading eyes to Lyn. 'I've been commissioned to do a complete refurbishing of the Pott's Point mansion that Mark Eden purchased recently. No expense spared. I'd like to show you the master bedroom.

He's stipulated a king-size bed, so it would require a special creation from you. Would you take it on?'

'I might. I'd like to see the room first,' Lyn answered cautiously, excited by the idea but looking to Peter for business guidance.

'Special work, special price,' he said promptly. 'There's having to see the job, putting up with you, Damien ...'

'Peter ...' Lyn's soft request begged him not to keep antagonising. She really wanted the job.

He grinned back at her and continued, completely unabashed, ticking off points on his fingers. 'Then there's job harassment, finding the perfect materials, the pressure of meeting a time schedule ...'

'No time problem,' Damien insisted. 'Eden doesn't want to take up occupation for another six months.'

'Ah, but inspiration can't be clocked,' Peter argued.

Damien heaved a sigh which expressed barely leashed temper. 'As I said, no expense spared. Within reason,' he added with more caution. 'I'd want a quotation before agreeing to the work.'

'Lyn will discuss the price after she's conceived the design,' Peter said decisively, then smiled. 'I know she will.'

'Well, we've settled everything here,' Damien declared, once more turning his considerable charm on to Lyn. 'Could I take you out to Pott's Point now to have a look at it?'

Lyn didn't know what to answer. She was eager to go, but there was Peter to consider. He'd come in her car and he might have something else planned for her. She looked questioningly at him, trying to contain her elation at this exciting turn of events. 'Am I free?'

He laughed. 'The only shackles to throw off are yours, Lyn.'

She smiled back at him, feeling wonderfully lighthearted. 'Then I'll go.'

'And so will I—off home. Give me your portfolio and the keys to the car. Damien can bring you home. Saves petrol.'

Damien frowned. 'Your home?'

Sheer devilment lit Peter's eyes. 'More or less. We have a neighbourly arrangement.'

'I see,' muttered Damien.

It was on the tip of Lyn's tongue to explain their neighbourly arrangement in firmer detail, but Peter forestalled her.

'I do hope so, Damien,' And there was teasing laughter in the eyes he turned to Lyn as he took her keys and portfolio. 'Have fun. That's what it's all about.' Then he swung back to Charles. 'Chalk this one up to me, Charles. The next favour's on you, mmm?' And on that note he made his exit, an irrepressible cavalier who laughed at life and all its sacred cows.

Lyn was suddenly assailed with a sharp sense of loss, followed by an even sharper sense of uncertainty. Could she handle the business with Damien Sinclair without Peter's support? He had carried her to this point, bolstering her confidence with his, and now she was not sure she was ready to stand alone . . . to be free.

Peter's words echoed in her ears, 'The only shackles to throw off are yours.' She could do it. Of course she could. Peter believed in her and she believed in herself. She was already a success, wasn't she? And her work was wanted by Damien Sinclair. She glanced at the very handsome man at her side and wondered why Peter didn't like him. The thought niggled her for a moment. Peter's perception of people was very shrewd, but maybe their antagonism was based on male competitiveness, which had nothing to do with her or her work, she assured herself complacently.

CHAPTER EIGHT

DAMIEN was all courteous charm, helping her out of the chair and carrying her coat for her when she decided against putting it on. She felt very warm under his admiring gaze. He led her to his estate car, apologised for the clutter of material samples in the back section, and saw her comfortably settled in the front passenger seat.

As he fastened his own seat belt Damien checked that her was properly in place, and Lyn was made extremely conscious of the way it slanted between her breasts, emphasising their shape. Again her nipples tingled into hardness under Damien's lingering gaze, and she was quite relieved when he turned aside to start the engine.

It was all very well to feel sexy and be considered sexy while Peter was at her side, but she did not feel so comfortable about it with Damien. She recalled Peter's mocking taunt, *Girls too easy for you, Damien?* Lyn did not want Damien Sinclair to consider her 'easy'. She wondered if he thought she was living with Peter and toyed with the idea of correcting any such false impression. Peter's comment had been misleading. Deliberately so? A hands-off warning?

She dismissed that idea. Peter had surely been indulging in his brand of mischief. She was free, he wanted her to be free. But to tell Damien Sinclair this would be hinting that she wanted his interest,

95

and although she found him very attractive physically she wanted to know more about him before giving him any go-ahead signals. After all, there must be some reason for Peter's dislike.

Once they were out in the traffic stream heading for the eastern suburbs, Damien threw her a friendly smile. 'I daresay you've been in many a mansion, Lyn.' The vivid blue eyes slanted an appeal. 'I may call you Lyn?'

'Yes, of course,' she answered quickly, not averse to the less formal address. 'And yes, I'm quite used to mansions, having lived in one most of my life. I don't recommend them as family homes,' she added dryly.

He laughed. 'I doubt if Mark Eden was thinking of family when he bought this one. He's all out to impress everyone.' He flicked her a warm, admiring glance. 'That's where you come in, Lyn. Your work will knock his eyes out.'

Pleasure brought a light flush to her cheeks. 'I'm glad you think so. Are you following any particular style on this job?' she asked, looking for guidance, a theme she might follow in her design.

Damien pulled a funny grimace. 'It's difficult. The mansion lends itself to the traditional. I'd love to fill it with antiques, but that wouldn't suit Mark Eden.'

Lyn nodded her understanding. Mark Eden was an entrepreneur on a grand scale, a flamboyant personality who seemed to have a finger in every big business takeover. He had made his first fortune in real estate, and his name was invariably connected to any large purchase in this area too, particularly tourist developments. When he entertained, it was a media occasion, full of spotlights.

'He showed me the paintings he's acquired,' Damien continued. 'Predominantly modern, striking and colourful. Fortunately the rooms have good natural light from tall windows. I'm keeping the furnishings light and in a subdued, modern fashion, with featured colour in the accessories. You'll get the idea when you see what I've done so far.' He threw her a wide grin. 'You could really let your head go with colour in the bedspread. He'd love it.'

Lyn smiled happily. 'That'll depend a little on the *en suite* rooms. Tell me about them.'

'No problem for you. The bathroom's white and gold and the dressing-rooms are mainly mirrored. White carpet.'

He chatted on about the various rooms he was in the process of redecorating, and Lyn found his company easy and his conversation stimulating. He asked her where she bought her fabrics and told her of several importers who regularly scouted the overseas markets. He himself had just returned from a buying trip to Europe and he described the latest trends in furnishings.

Tradesmen were leaving the mansion when Lyn and Damien arrived. A caretaker was busily closing and locking windows as Damien led her through the ground-floor rooms, which were in the process of being painted and papered. Lyn was impressed with the choices he had made.

'You have a very good eye for proportion and colour,' she remarked appreciatively.

He smiled. 'Coming from you that's some

compliment! Want to see the master bedroom now?'

'Yes, please,' she said eagerly.

His eyes grew warmer as he took her arm, and Lyn suddenly felt very conscious of his closeness. Although he had certainly been interested in her company she couldn't quite believe that he was attracted to her. A man as handsome as Damien would surely be looking for someone like Delvene, not Lyn. Yet that look in his eyes, and now he was putting his other hand over hers as he led her towards the staircase . . . her heart began to flutter.

'It's an impressive staircase,' she commented stiffly, telling herself not to be ridiculous. It was very flattering to think Damien might be attracted to her, but that was no reason for her imagination to start running riot. Just because Peter and bedrooms suggested sex, it certainly did not follow that Damien was like that.

'Yes. I wonder how many women have used it to stage an impressive entrance,' Damien mused softly.

Well, I'm not impressive, Lyn told herself, and put a stern damper on her over-active physical awareness. She switched her mind on to bedrooms and bedspreads. Anticipation lightened her step as Damien steered her to the master bedroom, and her eyes lit with avid interest when he opened the door and ushered her into a huge room.

The only furniture in it was the king-size bed, complete with an elegantly carved bedhead in pickled white, its detail picked out with gold. A row of French windows opened one wall out on to a balcony which overlooked the harbour. The predominantly white room was full of light and just begging for a bold splash of colour. Lyn made a quick check of the *en suite* rooms and found them just as Damien had described.

'You see?' Damien murmured as they moved back to the bedroom.

Her eyes sparkled up at him. 'I see. Did you have anything particular in mind?' she asked, careful not to assume too much.

For a moment Damien seemed amused by the hopeful uncertainty in her eyes. He cocked his head slightly to one side as if to study her better, paying particular attention to her mouth. Lyn's pulse thumped erratically. She had not been mistaken. He was attracted to her, and now she did not know if she wanted him to be. She was far too aware that they were alone in a bedroom. Damien's gaze dropped to her blouse, and her breath caught in her throat.

'I'm sure I'll want what you want,' he suggested softly.

With every nerve twanging tension Lyn decided that she had better put some discouraging distance between them. Fast. She walked over to the french windows and opened one to let in the cool breeze off the water. She liked Damien, and had enjoyed his company. But they were here to plan a bedspread and that was all she wanted from him at the moment. It was too soon for anything else. Still too . . . unbelievable.

'It's a lovely view, isn't it?' she remarked, wanting to break a silence which prickled at her uncomfortably.

'Lovely,' Damien echoed, coming up behind her. His hands slid round her waist and up, palms curving and rotating over her breasts in a movement so sensually exciting and shocking that it put Lyn in a state of paralysed confusion. She jerked her head towards him and a warm mouth claimed her ear, tongue-tickling it with an expertise which increased her shock. Her breath was trapped in a constricted throat and her heart was palpitating wildly. And she was horribly aware that her nipples were responding with telling prominence.

'You have the prettiest little breasts I've ever seen,' came the hot murmur in her ear. 'I've been wanting to touch them like this all afternoon. Touch all of you.'

His mouth trailed down her throat as his hands released her breasts and travelled downwards, over her stomach, pressing her back into him, then lower still, reaching her thighs and ricking her skirt upwards, fingers groping for the split-pleat. On a wave of panic Lyn gripped his hands hard, frustrating their purpose.

'I . . . I think you've got the wrong idea, Damien,' she choked out, twisting her head to evade his questing mouth.

'Then tell me your idea,' he murmured, swinging her round to face him, his hands smoothly fitting her body to his all-too-suggestive thrust. 'Anything with you would be exciting. You're an incredibly exciting woman.'

Her head swam with that thought until common sense reduced its power. 'No, I didn't mean . . .' she began frantically as his mouth hovered over hers, but any further words were effectively smothered.

Smothered, squashed and totally wiped away by his insistent possession.

And his hands were on her thighs again, gathering up her skirt. She struggled to release her arms, pinned to her side by his. She tried to lean back to break the kiss, but his head followed hers and she found herself thrust to an even more intimate awareness of his arousal. In desperation she wrenched her head aside.

'Stop it! Please stop!' she gasped.

'Why?' The deep voice was rough with desire. The blue eyes blazed down at her quivering mouth. 'Peter won't care if we ...'

'I care!' she shrilled at him.

A sharp frown shadowed the desire. His hold on her loosened. 'You're not in love with him? God, Lyn! You must know he doesn't give a damn about anything.'

She broke out of his embrace and backstepped out of easy reach, panting with distress from his physical mauling and agitatedly smoothing down her skirt. 'How dare you!' she choked out, then swallowed hard to gain voice. 'How dare you assume I'm anyone's plaything!'

'I didn't assume ...'

'Yes, you did!' she cut in with resentful fury.

'Lyn ...' His hands gestured appeal as he stepped towards her.

She backed away, stumbling against the door. 'Don't you come near me!' she shrilled. 'If this is what your job offer is about, then you can forget it!' Having regained her balance she swung on her heel and marched out, her small frame rigid with outraged dignity.

Damien caught up with her.

Lyn was too enraged even to glance at him. Peter had been right! Damien Sinclair was corrupt, all beautiful veneer and rotten within. How dared he think she was his for the taking just because ...? She flashed him a fierce look. 'For your information, I don't share Peter Kelso's bed. We're neighbours. And friends. And he wouldn't dream of—of forcing himself on me!'

She began stomping down the stairs, ignoring Damien who kept pace with her.

'Lyn, please listen to me. I didn't mean to upset you. Dammit all, I thought you felt the same as I did!'

She stopped to glare at him. 'What? A bit of lust for the afternoon? Does it give you a kick to sneak a lay with Peter's women? Is that some perverted kind of one-upmanship?'

That stung. 'Peter Kelso wouldn't hesitate over taking any woman of mine, so don't throw him in my face as a pillar of virtue,' he snarled.

'With one important difference, Damien. The woman would have some say in it.'

'Oh, to hell with Kelso!' he cursed savagely. 'He's got nothing to do with this.'

'Hasn't he just!' Lyn mocked just as savagely. 'It was you who brought him into it.'

'I'd want you any time on any terms.'

'Well, I don't happen to be on standby,' she flung back at him, and resumed stomping.

'And the job has nothing to do with it either. For God's sake! Will you listen to me?'

She stepped on to the marble floor of the spacious foyer and turned to confront him, her chin up and her eyes sparking with fiery pride. But for his mention of the job she would have kept on walking. He was, after all, Charles Sinclair's son, and common sense whispered that it was wiser to smooth over the ill feeling if that was possible.

'All right! I'm listening. But what you say had better be good, Damien, because I'm not feeling at all receptive. If you take my point.'

His grimace was a mixture of anger and frustration. 'About the job. I want you to do it. That is completely separate from any personal desires on my part, and I didn't anticipate that those desires would offend you so deeply. I'm sorry that I made a wrong assumption about your relationship with Peter Kelso, but you'd have to concede that his line of patter last night would lead anyone to that assumption.'

Heat scorched into Lyn's cheeks. 'That's just his way of talking,' she muttered defensively, although she had to admit Damien did have reason for his conclusion. 'But even if you thought I was sharing his bed, that doesn't give you licence to make free with my body. I'm my own person, and I'll thank you to respect me as such.'

Damien's expression softened to appeasement. 'I do respect you, Lyn. You have more creative talent than any woman I've ever met. I find that exciting. I find you exciting. I felt you were attracted to me and I acted on impulse. Is it so reprehensible that I should desire an exciting woman?'

Lyn's stony gaze wavered and fell. Damien had not been too wrong. She had been attracted to him. If he had not been so sexually aggressive she might even have been receptive to a kiss or two. But his mention of Peter had given a sordid flavour to the whole scene and she felt too disturbed by it to stay with him any longer. She lifted eyes which still held a shadow of revulsion. 'You had no right to force yourself on me as you did, whatever you thought. I want to go home, Damien.'

His eyes probed hers for some sign of softening. 'I really am sorry for distressing you. I didn't mean to, Lyn,' he said with every semblance of sincerity.

She nodded, embarrassed by the intimacies he had taken.

'I'll drive you home,' he murmured, and took her arm in a gentle hold.

Lyn was terribly self-conscious of her body and his as she walked beside him. When he handed her into the car it was a relief to be separated from him. He took his place behind the wheel but did not immediately switch on the ignition. Lyn tensed as he turned towards her, but his eyes were only projecting earnest appeal.

'Lyn, you will take the job?'

She still wanted it. Designing a bedspread for that room would be an exciting challenge. And she did not think Damien would try any sexual pressure on her again. 'I'll do a design. Then the decison's up to you, isn't it?' she answered guardedly.

His mouth curved into a wry smile. 'I can't imagine I'd be disappointed in your design.'

Meaning he was disappointed in her rejection of him? Lyn frowned and turned her face away. He started the engine. As they drove through the city she wondered if Damien could possibly be sincere in his protestations of interest in her. If he really had been strongly atttracted ...

'Have you been Peter's neighbour for very long, Lyn?'

The soft question cut across her thoughts. 'No, not long,' she answered slowly. 'Actually he's been my aunt's neighbour for the last ten years. They were good friends despite the large age difference between them. She died recently and I inherited her home unit.'

'Oh, I see,' Damien murmured.

That was what he had said when Peter had dropped the fact that they were neighbours. Lyn wryly wondered what Damien saw this time. The ensuing silence throbbed with the memories of what had passed between them.

'I hope you can accept my apology, Lyn. I wouldn't have . . .' He hesitated, then plunged on, his voice deeply intense. 'I'd like us to be friends, if that's still possible.'

Her heart lifted a little. Maybe he really was sincere. Time would tell anyway, and meanwhile it would make their working relationship easier if they could put this nasty incident behind them. 'I'd like that too,' she offered quietly.

His smile beamed relief and friendliness at her, and after a small hesitation Lyn smiled back.

Damien showed her every courtesy when they arrived at her apartment block, rushing to open the passenger door, escorting her to the lift and waiting for the doors to open so that he could hand her in. 'You'll let me know as soon as you have a design prepared?' he pressed anxiously.

She smiled. 'You can count on it. And thank you, Damien.'

'Thank you,' he replied with feeling.

Lyn rode up to the sixth floor, feeling relieved that the awkwardness was over. Now that the situation had been sorted out, she found it rather flattering to be in the position of being desired by two very desirable men. Not that Peter really counted, she reminded herself sternly, because she was not going to get involved with him beyond friendship. But as a friend he was marvellous. As for Damien ... well, he was very much a question mark after his behaviour today, but she was prepared to give him a second chance.

The elation of success returned as she let herself into her apartment. The telephone was ringing and she picked it up automatically, a smile still lingering on her lips.

'Lynette! Is that you?' Her mother's voice sounded shrill. And suspicious.

Here comes the condemnation, Lyn thought, and was surprised to find that the usual sick feeling in her heart did not immediately eventuate. She felt quite calm. Confident, free. 'Yes, it's me, Mother,' she answered matter-of-factly.

'Where have you been? I've called and called!' The voice was now hard and accusing.

'I've been out,' Lyn answered blithely. A totally uncharacteristic sense of mischief prompted her to ask, 'Is anything wrong?'

'Stop acting the innocent, Lynette!' Stern anger. 'You know what I'm ringing about. I warned you about that man. How could you demean yourself, and the family name, to be actually seen out with him? And Delvene said he suggested quite openly that he was having an affair with you!' Absolute outrage.

Delvene said. Normally Lyn cringed at those words, but today they had no power, none at all. 'I don't think that's true, Mother,' she said with a sang-froid which privately amazed her. 'What he actually said was that he would be pleased to have an affair with Delvene when I'm finished with him.'

A gasp of horror. 'Lynette! You're to pack up and come home immediately.'

Go back to that life? Never! Pure steel drove off Lyn's tongue. 'I'm sorry you're upset, Mother, but I assure you there's no reason to be. Peter Kelso has only been a kind, generous friend to me. He was merely teasing Delvene. He took me to the art show last night to meet Charles Sinclair. You know him, Mother. He owns Interiors of Distinction. Today Mr Sinclair bought three of my bedspreads and commissioned more. They're on display in his showroom now and he paid me twelve thousand dollars for them. So you see, I'm doing very well and there's no need for you, or Father, to worry about me.'

The steel had melted into a choking lump of emotion. Why hadn't her parents ever believed in her talent, encouraged her, helped her as Peter had? Why always the condemnation, just because she wasn't like Delvene?

There was a stony silence from the other end of the line. No pleasure in her success. No congratulations. Lyn summoned up the steel again. She didn't have to take this any more. That life was behind her, finished. But she couldn't repress an edge of bitterness as she rang down the final curtain on it.

'Please tell Father I won't be opening a shop. I know he'll be relieved. And tell Delvene she can still beat me to Peter Kelso's bed if she wants to. I haven't succumbed yet. I think that's all the good news. I'm very happy here and extremely busy and this is my home now. Goodbye, Mother.'

Still the stony silence. Slowly and sadly Lyn put the telephone down. In an instinctive act of self-determination she stiffened her spine and squared her shoulders. She did have value in her own right: Peter had assured her of that. And the Sinclairs had reinforced his judgement.

Peter . . . another, quite different emotion curled warmly round her heart. He had done more for her in two days, cared more for what she was and what she did, than her parents had ever done. Her involvement with him might carry penalties, but the prizes far outweighed them.

There was a casual rat-a-tat-tat on her door. Peter. She kicked off her high heels and skipped over to let him in. He had discarded his sartorial splendour and was dressed in shorts and a T-shirt on which was emblazoned, 'GO FOR IT'.

A smile twitched at her lips. He really was outrageous, but at least he was open and honest about it. He practised exactly what he preached, and although Lyn had laughed at his claim to integrity she did not doubt that he was indeed a man of integrity. In his own highly individual and eccentric fashion.

He grinned at her as he handed her the car keys and her portfolio. 'Just ordered some takeaway from Dial-a-dinner. Like to change the image and join me?'

There was no resisting his zany company. Quite simply he made Lyn feel it was good to be alive.

'Yes, I will,' she said emphatically.

One eyebrow rose. 'That sounds threatening. Had a wearing afternoon with the lap-pup?'

Lap-pup? Every last bit of tension from the afternoon drained away as Lyn burst into giggles. Damien had been lapping at her, and compared to Peter he was a pup. 'It was slightly wearing,' she gurgled, then with a spark of pride, 'but I did dictate my own terms at the end.'

Peter's eyes glowed with approval. 'You see? You didn't need me along. You're on your way, Lyn.'

'Thanks to you.'

He shook his head. 'I might have hastened the pace a little, but you've got what it takes. I think this calls for more champagne.'

Peter Kelso and champagne were too heady a brew. 'No, thanks. I'm only coming over for food and conversation,' she warned pointedly.

He grinned, his eyes full of teasing devilment. 'Your virtue is safe, my girl, until you give the word. Meanwhile, food and conversation it is. Always a pleasure to satisfy one appetite or another. My door is open to you.'

She laughed and shut her own door, in a hurry to change her clothes and be with him. She didn't care what anyone thought, she liked being with Peter Kelso. More than liked, she loved being with him. And Damien was wrong; Peter did care about some things. He had cared enough to help her. And he had cared about Aunt Henrietta. And even if he did rather dent her reputation, she could now stand up for herself against Delvene and her mother and Damien. And she'd won some respect for it too, which was all to the good.

She saw no reason why she shouldn't enjoy a friendship with Peter Kelso, similar to the friendship Aunt Henrietta had enjoyed with him. After all, he had declared that he wouldn't try to get her into his bed unless she asked him. And of course she would never ask. So there was no problem. None at all.

CHAPTER NINE

'I THINK I should start with your toes. Toes get so excited when properly handled. Imagine the tremendous little quivers of excitement running up your legs! Some women can have orgasms just through their toes—consider that! Isn't it marvellous?'

Lyn tried to shut him out of her mind and concentrate on her work, but Peter's banter continued to infiltrate.

'Now, if you could contain your excitement there, I'd show you what can be done with ankles. I love ankles, and yours are particularly dainty. Combine that with the soles of your feet, the wonderfully sensitive flesh behind the knees, and long, light caresses down the calves of your legs. Exquisite torture. Anyone who can undergo that without succumbing ...'

Lyn dragged her mind off toes and ankles and knees and heaved an exasperated sigh. 'Peter, please ... I'm trying to concentrate.'

The design for Mark Eden's bedspread was not coming out right. It had taken her three weeks to come up with a concept which satisfied her and the completed sketch was in front of her, almost covering her dining-room table. She was still sure that the design line was perfect, but something was wrong with the colours. She had cut out pieces of the fabrics she had intended using and placed them over the pencilled pattern. She turned her exasperation on them, unable to pinpoint what was causing her discontent.

'Or we could take a shower together,' Peter mused softly, enjoying his fantasies too much to desist altogether. 'Get to the same object from the other end, so to speak. Have you ever had your hair shampooed strand by strand? Thank God there are no excess water charges—I'd be a broken man! You could soap my manly chest while ...'

Strand by strand? The idea was ridiculous. 'Can't you be serious?' she tossed at him irritably.

'I am serious. Ah, I can see the problem now. Your shoulder muscles are all bunched up from leaning over that table. How about a good oil massage? I bought a bottle yesterday on the off chance that it would come in handy. Now, if I were doing an oil massage I'd start ...'

Her shoulders were stiff. Oh, good God! He really was a devil. She looked sternly at the figure so languidly stretched out in the most comfortable armchair, feet casually propped on the coffee table, a tantalising smile on his lips. 'You're not going to start,' she spelled out emphatically. 'Please let me concentrate. This isn't working.' She arched her back to relieve her muscles and dropped back into her chair, staring morosely at the pattern in front of her. Something was wrong, wrong, wrong.

Peter climbed to his feet and strolled across to look over her shoulder. He was granting her the silence she had demanded, but Lyn was terribly aware of his closeness. Toes, showers and oil massages flitted through her mind, one titillating temptation after another.

Sometimes she wished he would actually make a move, draw her into an embrace, kiss her until she was senseless, seduce her in earnest. But he never did. Whenever he touched her it was only in a friendly fashion, not even taking the slightest intimacy over which she could take umbrage—or encouragement. Damn him! She was not going to ask him to take her to bed. Never! He could get his exercise elsewhere. Not with her.

His hand dropped casually on to her shoulder as he leaned forward. His fingers rested lightly on her skin, no caress, no massage. Yet the flesh beneath that passive touch was alive with sensitivity, waiting, wanting, almost screaming for positive activity. Lyn clenched her teeth against the impulse to ask, and cursed the weakness which silently begged Peter to take the initiative, to take the decision away from her.

He pointed to one of the fabrics. 'For the last half-hour I've thought it was the aqua,' he murmured. 'Should be a deeper tone. But I could be wrong.'

Lyn's eyes stared at the fabric unseeingly for a moment. The aqua, her mind echoed. A deeper tone. She wrenched her thoughts away from the hand on her shoulder and focused all her concentration on the design in front of her. Yes. Yes, that was it. Peter had put his finger on the trouble spot with unerring judgement. If she used a deeper tone there, it would throw up the contrast of the violet and ... yes, it would be as she had envisaged it. She looked up at Peter, eyes shining with happy relief. 'You're right.'

'And now let's talk about love,' he said with smug satisfaction. 'Or flying off to a remote Pacific island

to look at tapa as an inspiration for your designs. Or
entering a car in Le Mans next year. Or skiing down
the slopes of Switzerland. But making love is the
best idea.'

She forced a laugh which sounded tinny even to
her ears. She broke it off and spoke quickly,
defensively. 'You aren't talking about love, Peter
Kelso. You're talking about exercise.' But she
wished he was talking about love. Wished it quite
desperately. And just as desperately she hid the
vulnerability in her heart.

His thumb fanned a taut neck muscle before his
hand dropped away. 'You let yourself get too
uptight, Lyn. You really could do with some
exercise and relaxation. You know why you didn't
pick up that tone just now?'

'Because you were deliberately distracting me,'
she accused, trying to shrug off the physical
awareness which was still prickling at her.

'Not at all. You've gone stale. You've been
working flat out for three weeks. Not good for the
mind or the body. No fun.'

'But it has been fun,' she protested, swivelling
round in her chair to face him. 'I've loved every
minute of it.'

He folded his arms and his mobile face assumed a
musing expression. 'Why is it that I always dote on
obsessional women? I see all this intense energy
being poured out and it excites me. I think to
myself—what would it be like to have it all directed
on to me? If I released the full force of her
powerhouse of passion? My God! What a glorious
peak to climb! Beyond ecstasy.'

For a moment Lyn was caught up in his fantasy.

Would she be a powerhouse of passion under Peter's expert stimulation? Then she brought herself down to earth with a thump. And be marked up as another novel experience in his life of novelty? Every instinct told her she would want to hang on, have it continue, herself and Peter together always. And that was a fantasy which had no hope of coming true. He was a free spirit and no one was ever going to shackle him.

She jumped up from her chair and picked up the cup of coffee he had brought her. In her anxiety over the design she had forgotten all about it and the coffee was stone cold. 'I think I'll make some fresh. Want another cup?' she asked with forced brightness.

He rolled his eyes. 'And she accuses me of having no soul!'

'I didn't say that at all. You've got one. You just keep it to yourself,' she retorted airily. 'But that's all right so long as you don't expect to feed off mine. I'll satisfy my passions in my own way, and that isn't your way, Peter.'

He sighed. 'The confidence of the ignorant! You haven't tried it yet. But it's only been three weeks. Hope springs eternal. The time will come.'

But it mustn't come, Lyn told herself sternly. She wanted love, needed the commitment of love. If she gave herself to Peter and then he lost interest in her she would die. So it mustn't ever come to that.

She made the coffee and they took it out to the balcony. Peter had made a habit of wandering over in the evening if her light was still on. He'd announce that it was suppertime and he would stay and talk for a while. Sometimes he'd ask her to join him for a takeaway dinner which he had had delivered. Sometimes Lyn cooked and reciprocated his hospitality.

She was fascinated by the range of his knowledge and the breadth of his vision. His opinions were backed by insight and a wealth of experience. But overlaying all this was the sexual banter, and Lyn was convinced now that he really did want her. And she wanted him. It should have been simple, but it wasn't, because she needed more than Peter would ever be prepared to give. And the need was mounting every day. Somehow she had to reduce the pressure, the temptation.

'Why don't you go off to Switzerland and ski down the slopes? You obviously have the time,' she suggested halfheartedly, needing a breathing-space yet not wanting him to leave her.

'Ah, but not the inclination. Unless you come with me.' His eyes warmed her with their invitation. 'Will you?'

She shook her head. 'I'm too busy.'

'You know what they say about all work and no play . . .'

She sighed. 'Well, if I get dull, I'm sure you'll tell me. But seriously, Peter, why don't you take off for a holiday somewhere?'

He looked at her in a way that jolted her heart and made her pulse race chaotically.

'Because all the excitement I want is right here,' he answered quietly.

Lyn quickly turned her head away and took a deep breath to calm the chaos inside her. Excitement. The excitement of the chase. But she mustn't let him overtake her. Once he had won she would be like all the rest of the women in his life.

Lyn had not actually seen any women coming to and going from Peter's apartment since the first morning with Jessie Talbot. But then, she had hardly kept a watch for them. It was highly unlikely that Peter had turned celibate all of a sudden. She wished ... but it was no use wishing he was any different from what he was. He wouldn't then be Peter Kelso.

'You know, you haven't told me anything about your family,' she remarked questioningly, feeling a sharp need to understand the forces which had shaped his character.

His eyes twinkled mischief. 'I'm a visitor from outer space, tasting the delights of this world before passing on to the next.'

She brushed aside his nonsense. 'I want to know, Peter.'

He sighed. 'I have a very considerate family who've never interfered in anything I've wanted to do. My mother has a tremendous zest for life. A marvellous person in her own right. I've set her up in the hotel she wanted on the Gold Coast and she's in her element there. She has been, and I'm sure always will be, a barmaid who takes joy in cheering up her customers.'

He pulled a wry grimace. 'My father is almost the direct opposite, a very self-contained fellow who rarely considers his fellow man. He lectures in an institute at Canberra—professor of mathematics. The only spice he's ever had in his life was when he formed the habit of co-habiting with my mother once a week. It pleased my mother to cheer him up and she was mightily impressed with his mind.'

'They ... they weren't married?' Lyn asked tentatively.

Peter's eyebrows waggled at her, mocking her conventional train of thought. 'No, my mother didn't fancy the idea of any man running her life. Liked making her own decisions and doing as she pleased. It pleased her to have a child, and she figured my father was a suitable partner in that particular enterprise. She's a very astute woman. With the mathematical ability I inherited from him and her penchant for gambling, she and I made a great team.'

A smile of affection curved his lips. 'Actually I'm quite fond of my father too. His view of life is very narrow, but he's always taken a paternal interest in me and paid for whatever education I wanted. I'm the only family he has. He still spends occasional weekends with my mother. They're quite fond of each other, but in small doses. End of story.'

It was quite an extraordinary story, but Lyn decided that it fitted him. Such an extraordinary person had to have been shaped from an extraordinary background. 'Did you ever mind being illegitimate?' she asked curiously.

'Good God, no!' He laughed at the idea. 'Life with my mother was so great that I used to pity my more conservatively controlled schoolmates. Not that my mother doesn't have very firm rules about behaviour towards others. She's kindness itself. But what makes her such fun to be with is that she invariably greets every morning with the happy conviction that it will bring some new excitement.'

'Like you,' Lyn smiled.

Peter cocked a cheeky eyebrow at her. 'I go one

step further and make something exciting happen.'

'And what did you make happen today?'

He grinned his triumph. 'Among other things I helped you finish your design.'

Lyn's smile turned a little wry. 'Was that exciting?'

'Wasn't it?'

'Yes, it was,' she agreed on a sigh, wishing that the other excitement he promised so temptingly could be made into something as lasting as the bedspread would be. But Peter was like his parents, not seeking or needing emotional ties. Lyn set her wayward thoughts back on to business. 'How much do you think I should ask for this bedspread?'

'Mmm . . . a base of eight thousand and the same terms as the others as far as the mark-up is concerned.'

Lyn's eyebrows shot up. 'I thought maybe six thousand. Are you sure eight's not too much? It's not really double the work, Peter.'

'Chickenfeed for Mark Eden. Besides, he's used to paying big money for works of art. He'll reckon he's got a bargain. And he will have. Damien will probably bill him for twenty—that's why the mark-up percentage is so important. Stops him from cheating you. Damien has always had an eye out for the main chance.'

Lyn frowned. Damien had been quick to seize the chance to try having sex with her. But afterwards he had seemed genuine in his feelings towards her. Or had that merely been a smoothing-over process because he wanted to do business with her without any hostility getting in the way? She wondered how he would act towards her at their next meeting, and a sense of anticipation was awakened. Now that the design was finalised she could telephone him tomorrow.

Friends. That was Damien's proposition, but could a man and woman be nothing but friends when there was a strong sexual attraction? Peter was gradually undermining her resolve not to go to bed with him. She thought about it far too often for her peace of mind. Not that it was all she wanted, but it was all Peter was offering. It was always there . . . the waiting for her to give in. And he made the idea so wickedly attractive. But she couldn't take that step. It would surely cement her need for him. Then where would she be when he wanted to be free?

Perhaps a friendly relationship with Damien could help counteract the insidious effects of the temptations Peter kept throwing at her. The distraction of another man's interest might be precisely what she needed. She had become too dependent on Peter's company, too aware of him.

'You've gone very silent. Thinking of bed?' he teased lightly.

All too true, but Lyn determinedly evaded the trap. 'Mm, my own. I feel drained.'

He sighed. 'Maybe it's fingers and hands and arms and elbows that turn you on. Elbows are very kinky. Next time I'll talk about elbows.' He got up and smiled down at her. 'I should wish you the sleep of the unjust, but I'm too kind. Good night, Lyn.'

'Good night, Peter. Thanks for the advice.'

'One of these nights you'll take it,' came the dry retort.

He took a step away, paused, then stepped back,

his hand lightly falling on her shoulder. She glanced up questioningly. His expression had lost all trace of amusement. The dark eyes probed hers carefully.

'You do know you're very special to me, Lyn,' he said softly, half statement, half question. 'One of a kind.'

Her heart turned over. 'I thought you said I was like Aunt Henrietta,' she said defensively.

His mouth quirked a little. 'There were some things I didn't want to share with Old Henry.'

Like his bed. Lyn dragged her gaze from his mouth and stared blindly out over the harbour. She might be special to him. She might even be one of a kind. That didn't mean he would want her for a lifetime. 'Good night, Peter,' she said decisively.

There was a light finger pressure on her shoulder, then his touch was withdrawn. 'Good night, Lyn,' he murmured.

He took himself off without another word but his presence lingered on, tormenting Lyn with all that she had denied. She was so terribly close to succumbing to Peter's fascination. Somehow she had to distance herself from the temptation, and perhaps Damien Sinclair could provide the means.

Damien certainly sounded eager when Lyn telephoned him the next day. He suggested he should drop into her apartment at five o'clock the following afternoon, thus saving her the trouble of carting the large design to the store for him to see. Peter drew up a contract for her and said she need only knock on his door when she wanted him. For his signature. Or anything else.

Lyn decided she need not dress quite so professionally for this business visit, but she was conscious of a desire to look attractive without being overtly sexy. She settled on her best white slacks and a cotton overblouse which she had screen-painted at art school. The mauve, tan and white pattern was unusual and striking, and she felt very pleased with her appearance when Damien arrived and looked admiringly at her.

His visual impact had lost nothing, despite his behaviour at the Pott's Point mansion. He looked more handsome than ever in a dark brown business suit. Lyn could not help wondering if he still found her desirable. Not that she wanted him to desire her—at least, not to the extent of physical force— but it was certainly flattering that a man who could make any woman drool over his looks should be attracted to her.

Damien enthused over the Mark Eden design with such eloquent pleasure that Lyn warmed to the admiration in his eyes. He agreed to the price Peter had recommended without turning a hair, and was equally agreeable about signing the contract and writing her out a deposit cheque. Lyn had just about forgiven him his past indiscretion and was heading for the door to fetch Peter to act as witness to the contract when Damien put out a hand to detain her.

'Lyn . . .' The blue eyes were soft with persuasive appeal. 'If you haven't anything planned for tonight, would you come out to dinner with me? It's not just to express my appreciation for the work you've done. I'd really like to get to know you. If not tonight, then perhaps another night?'

Lyn hesitated. She did like Damien. He was offering her a chance to escape the physical spell Peter was weaving round her, but she could not ignore the fact that he had been far more physical than Peter had ever been. There was no point in running away from a sexual relationship by plunging herself along the path of another one. What she needed was a breathing space. The hand on her forearm slid down to her fingers, startling her out of her intense reverie.

'I'm not stupid, Lyn,' Damien said quietly.

The light stroke of his thumb across her palm made her skin tingle, but it was only a pleasant tingle, nothing alarming. Even if Damien should try to make love to her, he was resistible.

His smile was all charm. 'I'm asking for the chance to show you I can be a gentleman.'

Why not give it to him? Lyn thought quickly. One night of a gentlemanly Damien could be very pleasant. Pleasantly distracting, if nothing else. And for all she knew it could be the beginning of a relationship which might develop more solid foundations than anything she could have with Peter. She had enjoyed Damien's company before he had been ... ungentlemanly.

'All right, I'd like that, Damien. Thank you.'

'Tonight? After we've cleared away the business with the contract?' he pressed eagerly.

Why not? There was no reason to put him off now that the decision had been made. 'You'll have to wait until I change into something more suitable.'

He smiled his delight. 'Happy to wait!'

Lyn went across the hallway to summon Peter, feeling strangely at odds with herself. But she was free to go out with Damien, wasn't she? Peter would be the first person to tell her she was free to do whatever she wanted. But she did not feel right about the situation as her hand automatically copied Peter's rat-a-tat-tat knock on his door.

He answered promptly, dressed in shorts and another T-shirt, this one featuring a nun-like Julie Andrews and a message which shouted, CLIMB EVERY MOUNTAIN. Lyn gave a rueful smile as she delivered her own message.

'You mean to say there are no mountains to climb?' Peter demanded in mock disappointment.

'Everything agreed,' she assured him. And he was not going to conquer her either, she silently determined. That was all she would be, a sexual conquest.

'How dull!' he muttered as they crossed to her apartment, but his humour was instantly restored as he saw Damien. 'Ah, Damien ... modelling the forefront of fashion again. Following my lead, I see.'

Damien raised a mocking eyebrow at the T-shirt. 'Not exactly, Peter.'

'Well, don't be wasting our time now. Since you're intent on signing, sign and be off with you.' Peter flourished a pen. The signatures were quickly taken care of, and as Peter scrawled his name for the last time he remarked, 'You really should marry Lyn, Damien. It'd save you money in the long run.'

'I might very well take an option on that idea,' Damien replied, the blue eyes twinkling flirtatiously at Lyn.

Peter cocked an eyebrow at him. 'Be bold. Ask her now.'

'Peter ...' muttered Lyn threateningly. Marriage might be a mocking matter to him, but Lyn did not care for this particular levity.

'Bad luck, dear boy. She doesn't want you. Better paddle off and play elsewhere.' He grinned at her, his face alight with all sorts of mischief. 'Lyn and I have to celebrate the upturn in her fortunes.'

She checked a stab of disappointment. It would have been fun celebrating with Peter, but the memory of her last celebration with him was still sharp in her mind. He was closer to her now. Dangerously close. Which was why she was going out with Damien.

'I'm sorry, Peter, I can't. Not tonight.'

'Lyn's accepted my invitation to dinner,' Damien put in with a touch of smugness.

For a fleeting moment the mischief was snuffed out. The dark eyes darkened at Lyn. Then in the flick of an eyelid a gleam appeared. He turned to Damien in arch surprise. 'Well, aren't you going to ask me too? Where's your gratitude, man? Your sense of what's right and proper?'

'Where Lyn is concerned I feel distinctly selfish,' replied Damien, a very cold rejection in his voice.

'Aha! Doesn't want a chaperon, eh?' Peter switched to Lyn. 'Are you going to risk falling into his clutches? Don't you want me there to shield you from unbridled lust?'

Lyn hesitated. It was not so much the reminder of her previous experience with Damien as the tone Peter had used. The uncharacteristic edge to his banter had struck her sharply. He did not want her to go with Damien. Was he jealous? Did he care enough to want to keep her to himself? Or did he simply think that Damien would take advantage of her? That was the most probable answer.

'I think I can escape his clutches for one night,'

she said dryly, ignoring the sickness in her heart.

Peter shook his head. 'Better put on your chastity belt, Lyn. He's not like me.' He strolled to the door and looked back at her. The gleam of devilment had winked out. The darkness was back—opaque, expressionless. 'If you ever need help again, you know where to find me.'

And he was gone. The door shut with a click of finality. Lyn stared at it, suddenly afraid that he wasn't coming back, ever. At least, not without her asking. And she could not ask, because asking meant . . .

'He's wrong, Lyn.'

Damien's voice penetrated her agonised thoughts. She looked blankly at him. 'What?'

The vivid blue eyes poured forth reassurances. 'I promise you won't need a chastity belt.' And he smiled as the ridiculous term passed his lips, inviting a responsive smile from her.

Did she want to go out with Damien? At the cost of losing Peter? But Peter wasn't hers to lose. It was all a game to him, just a game. And she would be hurt if she played it. Better for the game to be over now before it finished his way. Damien was not so dangerous to her. She forced a smile.

'I won't be long. Would you like a drink while I'm changing?'

Relief relaxed his stance. 'No, thanks. I'm quite happy to stand here and drink in your design.'

Her smile became less forced. 'I won't be more than ten minutes.'

Lyn put on her rose outfit. It gave her a veneer of confidence. Inside she was a mess of churning emotion. But Peter had wanted her to be free, hadn't he? Not tied to him? He didn't believe in ties. It had been all right by him that first day when she went off with Damien. Why not tonight?

But it was different; it was no use fooling herself it wasn't different. It broke the sense of sharing which had pulsed between her and Peter, pulling her towards his bed. And that could not have gone on or she would have succumbed. So she was right to break it, walk away from the game before it broke her.

Peter had walked away. He had not really tried to persuade her from going out with Damien. He did not like it, but he had not cared enough to make a strong stand. He had left her with her own choice. And her inner desolation told her it was the right choice. The desolation would be a thousand times worse if she ever went to bed with Peter, because he would walk away from that too. Once a mountain had been climbed, Peter Kelso would be looking for another to excite him.

And Damien? Lyn could not really foresee any future with him. He was almost too handsome to be real. But he wanted her company tonight. And she needed his.

CHAPTER TEN

'THE effect you've created with that dress is nothing short of sensational,' Damien said with admiration when Lyn finally presented herself.

'Thank you.' Her smile needed little forcing this time. Damien's appreciation of her work gave them some common ground, and she determined to put Peter completely out of her mind and enjoy the evening ahead.

Unfortunately they had only just stepped out of her apartment and were waiting for the lift when Damien himself undermined her purpose. 'I'm glad you stood up to Kelso,' he commented smugly. 'The man is insufferable and needs to be put down.'

Lyn could barely contain an instant leap to Peter's defence and an equally hot resentment at Damien's self-satisfaction. Her mind seethed with dissent. She owed so much to Peter. He had helped her when she needed help, stood by her when she was alone, been kind and thoughtful and supportive in countless ways.

But for her own frightening vulnerability to his strong attraction, she would be with him now, and the impulse to throw Damien's invitation back in his face and go to Peter was so compelling that only the lift's arrival swung the balance towards keeping her resolve.

All the same, she did not like Damien thinking that her acceptance of his company was a personal score off Peter. It made her feel disloyal, but she couldn't very well point out that she was not so much drawn to Damien's attractions as running away from Peter's. She had made her choice, the only sensible choice, and her sense of fairness demanded that she should now give Damien a reasonable trial.

The trial was over almost before it had begun. Damien took control of all the talking. As they drove to their destination he regaled Lyn with all his past achievements, his present masterpieces in the making, and his future, grandiose ambitions. It was the ultimate ego trip, and Lyn's receptivity quickly reached saturation point and passed beyond.

Her thoughts wandered back to Peter. Not once had she ever been bored by his conversation. Shocked, sometimes, but it was the shock of the unexpected. Peter was always challenging her preconceived ideas, provoking her into thinking differently. And she was beginning to think like him, more and more. Damien was a deadly bore, an egomaniac who stood absolutely no chance of answering the emotional dilemma that Peter presented to her.

'Weren't you listening to me?'

The sharp irritation in Damien's voice cut across her thoughts. 'Of course,' she replied quickly, throwing him a conciliatory smile and hoping he would repeat the point at issue.

'I consider it one of my best achievements, but I'd

like your opinion,' he said in a mollified tone.

'Certainly,' Lyn agreed, wondering what on earth he was talking about. She didn't want to offend him.

'Here we are!' he announced, nodding towards the neon sign which spelled 'HUBERT'S'.

It was the 'in' restaurant, having won a cult following amongst the gourmet set over the past year. It had inevitably ensured a fashionable following by placing its culinary delights in the upper price bracket. Aware of how expensive the place was, Lyn appreciated the compliment Damien was paying her. She tried once more to give him her full attention.

'Haven't you been here before?' he asked a little testily.

Lyn frowned, wishing she knew what he wanted from her. Clearly she had failed to give the right response. 'No, I haven't. But my sister has. She said the food was superb,' she added brightly.

'She didn't comment on the décor?'

'No. At least I can't recall her remarking on it.'

Damien's annoyance cleared to a pacified smile. 'Well, I'm sure you have a more perceptive eye than your sister.'

The décor! That was it! Damien's work. Lyn smothered a little sigh of relief. She hadn't completely fluffed her lines. Having accepted his invitation, the least she could do was pay him the courtesy of listening to him. Her upbringing demanded that good manners should be kept to the fore.

No sooner had Damien led her into the restaurant than his arms swept out in major-domo fashion, demanding a reaction. 'Don't you think it's the perfect setting for a class restaurant?'

No, was Lyn's instant but hastily choked off reply. The décor was stark: black suede chairs in a modern, functional style, starched white linen tablecloths, a chrome and glass bar which did not invite resting elbows. The washed-out apricot toning in the carpet was repeated in full gloss paint on the walls and ceiling, and the silver-framed black and white sketches hanging on the walls did nothing to alleviate the clinical mood of the place. Lyn searched frantically for a tactful answer. 'It's ... very ... striking.'

It was not enough. Damien wanted more. 'Don't you love it?' he persisted with self-centred blindness.

It had about as much appeal to Lyn as a hospital corridor, but the furniture was expensive and the sketches were fine pieces of art, and certainly the décor was all in character. Soulless character. If this was what Damien had set out to achieve, he had achieved it. 'It's perfect, Damien. You're a genius.'

He swallowed her acclaim as if it were strawberries and cream. It was not until the head waiter had settled them at a table that he revealed why her approval had been mandatory. 'Of course, Kelso doesn't have the taste to appreciate what I've done here. He made some rather cutting public statements about it. I'm glad you haven't let him get close to you, Lyn. The man has no soul.'

'I wouldn't go so far as to say that,' Lyn said dryly.
She loved the way Peter had furnished his apartment, and a more telling contrast to this ...
nothing-place she could not imagine.

'Oh, he's not so blind that he can't see the
obvious, as in your work, Lyn,' Damien conceded
with a touch of arrogant patronage. 'But this ...
the man can't appreciate the class of simplicity.
Vulgar opulence is his style.'

Sensual opulence, perhaps, Lyn thought, but
nothing the least bit vulgar. However, she refrained
from comment. Damien's bias left no room for
argument. But her good manners were strained.

A waiter handed them large handwritten menus,
and Lyn hid a secret little smile behind hers. She
would have loved to ask Damien what Peter had
said about the décor. She would have bet anything
that his opinion had been a straight reflection of her
own.

Lyn's good manners were strained further when
Damien took it upon himself to order her meal
without even bothering to consult her. 'As a
delicacy you can't beat the sole quenelles, and the
pheasant with the spinach stuffing is incomparable.
You must have it,' he told her, as if his superior
judgement was beyond question.

It was the same with the wine. 'I only ever drink
Burgundy,' he announced smugly. 'I actually visited
the vineyards when I was in France. Do you know
the Burgundians have been planting their vines in
the same soil for over two thousand years? They
literally live their wine twenty-four hours of the day.

Never think or talk of anything else. When I was there ...'

They were served a complimentary glass of champagne and a small plate of hors d'oeuvre while Damien raved on, airing knowledge which might have been interesting if he had had any real feeling for the Burgundians and their customs.

Lyn watched him talk, noting how very aware he was of himself, using his hands and eyes and mouth to focus attention on their fineness. She understood now why Peter could not resist mocking him. All veneer, no substance, he had said, and Lyn was ready to agree that the only substance was hot air.

His monologue came to an abrupt halt, his gaze drawn and held by something of startling interest. Lyn glanced round to see Delvene standing in the restaurant foyer, her arm linked to an escort but her gaze linked to Damien's. Surprise was stamped on her beautiful face.

No doubt she was astonished to find her younger sister in the company of such a stunningly handsome man, Lyn thought with amusement. And for the first time in her life she was glad to see Delvene. She actually wanted her sister to sweep in and take over her man. Indeed, it would suit her very well if Delvene and Damien devoured each other, relieving her of any duty to courtesy.

But an odd look of wariness was clouding the interest on Delvene's beautiful face. Apparently her experience with Peter, and Lyn's subsequent defiance at her last take-over attempt, was still a sharp memory. She was not sure that Lyn would be the doormat of the past. The green gaze flicked to Damien again, beauty attracting beauty. Lyn gave her an encouraging wave.

'That's my sister,' she informed Damien.

He dragged his eyes back to her, astonishment filming the glitter of admiration. 'Your sister! My God! You're not at all alike. She's so . . .'

'Perfect,' Lyn finished dryly, not at all pained by the tactless gaffe. Which was another first. 'Shall I call her over? It would be nice to dine together, don't you think?' she suggested, and was conscious of a heady sense of power as the suggestion was eagerly accepted. This time she was in control. Like Peter. Manipulating the moves.

Delvene's first reaction to Lyn's call was hesitation, a hint of suspicion. Lyn had never sought her company. Nevertheless, Damien's attraction overrode the hesitation, just as Lyn had known it would.

Introductions were politely interchanged, and with absolute predictability Delvene accepted the invitation to join Lyn and Damien, not even bothering to consult her escort's wishes on the matter. Lyn felt a stab of guilty sympathy for the man, but he quickly disposed of her momentary qualm. Steve Hanson's first conversational gambit showed him to be on a superficial par with Damien.

'Splendid place, this. Real class. Top food. And all the best people as clientèle,' he beamed.

'You haven't been here before, have you, Nettie?' Delvene asked in a pose of sisterly interest.

Nettie! Lyn smiled as she recalled Peter's inspired example of how to handle her sister's bitchy-sweet condescension. 'No, I haven't, Delly.'

Delvene's mouth tightened.

Lyn blithely continued speaking as if she hadn't noticed the reaction. 'The décor is Damien's work. He brought me here to get my opinion of it. I'm sure he'd like to hear yours.'

Delvene gushed enthusiastic compliments. Damien swelled with pride, and proceeded to demonstrate his authority on all things decorative, his authority on everything, the food, the wine, any subject that Lyn slyly introduced. It was like creating a play, and Lyn sat back and watched the performance with cynical amusement.

But the amusement grew more and more empty and Lyn's detachment became stronger as the evening wore on. She was the outsider at the feast, just as she had been all her life. Except with Peter. Peter . . . the one and only person who had reached into her mind, plucking out what she was thinking and feeling with an ease of understanding which she loved. Any activity with Peter was a pleasure, even the most mundane chore like washing up dishes.

'Lyn . . .' Delvene had not once repeated the hated 'Nettie'. 'I was just saying to Damien how glad I am that you've dropped that dreadful Peter Kelso. Mummy has been terribly worried about you. She'll be so relieved when I tell her you were out with a real gentleman.' She flashed Damien a dazzling smile.

'Lyn only associated with him for business reasons,' Damien put in pompously.

'Oh, I'm sure that's all it was,' Delvene agreed

quickly, innocence personified.

Lyn couldn't resist the impulse to throw the cat amongst the puffed-up pigeons. 'It amazes me how people leap to such false assumptions when all the evidence points in another direction,' she said with dry emphasis.

Delvene shot a startled look at her. 'You can't mean . . .? You wouldn't do anything which would let that man embarrass the family, Lyn?'

Damien gave a bark of derisive laughter. 'That's certainly Kelso's speciality—embarrassing every-one he can! But Lyn gave him short shrift this afternoon when he tried it on her, so you can tell your family they have nothing to worry about, Delvene.'

Lyn's hackles rose. 'Damien's quite correct, I did give Peter short shrift this afternoon, much to my regret. I should have asked him along with us tonight. The evening would have been immeasur-ably enhanced by his presence.'

Damien and Delvene gaped at her.

Lyn continued with icy deliberation. 'I happen to consider Peter Kelso the kindest person I've ever known, the truest friend I've ever had, and a man of the greatest integrity. I would always be proud to be associated with him. In any capacity,' she affirmed with feeling as she rose to her feet.

The sweet course had not yet been served, but Lyn had had enough. Their self-satisfied condem-nation of Peter was the last straw. You only live once, she said to herself, accepting Peter's philo-sophy, and she was not going to fritter away any

more of her time with such petty, shallow people.
And to hell with good manners!

'I'm going home now,' she stated with sublime
indifference to their reactions. 'Please feel free to
stay, Damien, I have no wish to cut short your
pleasure. Good night to you all.'

She swept them a polite smile, turned on her heel
and walked away, serenely dignified in her decision
and not the least bit perturbed by the confusion she
left behind. She was free of all that. Free, as Peter
was free, striding her own path, doing what she
wanted to do.

When Damien caught up with her on the street
she was intensely irritated by his conventional
outrage. It was so self-defeating. He should have
stayed where he really wanted to be, instead of
getting himself all fussed. And fussing her. 'What
the devil do you think you're doing?' he demanded.

'I told you what I was doing,' Lyn retorted
reasonably. 'Go on back to Delvene, Damien. Have
yourself a ball.'

'So that's it! You're jealous.'

Jealous! Lyn almost laughed at the absurdity of
the claim.

'Look, I'm sorry if I seemed to be paying too
much attention to your sister. I didn't realise I was
upsetting you. I assure you . . .'

'I'm not jealous,' Lyn cut in impatiently. 'You're
welcome to Delvene. It's why I invited her to our
table. You're welcome to stay with her all night.
Just go back there and get on with it. I simply want
to go home.'

'Then I'll take you,' Damien huffed with equal impatience. 'You think I'd let you walk off on your own?'

No, that wouldn't fit Damien's image of himself, Lyn realised, and resigned herself to being delivered home by him. He led her to his car in a cloud of displeasure. Once on their way he set himself to soothing her supposed umbrage at the attention he had given Delvene. Lyn sighed. He just couldn't believe that she didn't care.

'Damien, I'm really not interested,' she cut in bluntly. 'Nor am I offended by your very natural attraction to Delvene. To be perfectly frank with you, I think the two of you are well suited. My going out with you was a mistake. Now, please, just let it go.'

'It's Kelso, isn't it?' Damien flung at her resentfully. 'You've let that bastard get to you.'

Lyn disdained to answer. She was not prepared to discuss Peter with Damien.

'Well, let me tell you, you're one in an endless queue to Kelso. Just another bit of tail for him to . . .'

'That's enough!' Lyn cried defensively.

'Enough? I haven't even begun,' Damien sneered. 'He's not cutting me out again. It made me sick, hearing you stand up for him. Now you're going to hear . . .'

'Cutting you out!' Lyn sliced in with scorn. 'Is that why you were so attracted to me, Damien? Thinking you could score one off Peter?'

'Of course not,' he denied vehemently. 'I don't go

for any woman unless I want her myself.'

Maybe he had wanted her, but not deeply enough to withstand Delvene's superficial attraction. 'Forget it, Damien,' she advised him wearily. 'I'm sorry, but I realise now that I shouldn't have accepted your invitation. The only involvement I want with you is a business involvement; however, I'd prefer to part from you tonight on peaceable terms. Who knows? You might form a relationship with my sister. And nothing you can say will affect what I think of Peter.'

But it hurt her. She hated being reminded of Peter's record with women. Her heart writhed with the conflict of wanting him, as so many other women had wanted him and would undoubtedly want him in the years ahead.

Damien said no more. Whether it was the reminder of business or the suggestion about Delvene, Lyn didn't know or care. It was enough that some awakened sense of discretion had forced him to swallow his bile. They completed the trip home in silence and exchanged polite goodbyes as Lyn alighted from the car, having firmly declined Damien's cold offer to see her to her door.

She shrugged off the whole regrettable encounter. It was not worth thinking about. Peter claimed all her thoughts. She stepped into the lift and pressed the button for the top floor. The memories of all the times she had shared this tiny space with Peter crowded into her mind. Her feeling for him had come a long, long way from the antagonism which had accompanied that first ride down to the garage to unpack her car.

The lift jerked to a halt and Lyn stepped out on to the floor she shared with Peter, knowing that she wanted to share everything with him. Her gaze was inevitably drawn to his door as she privately acknowledged what she had refused to admit to herself for so long. She loved Peter Kelso, loved him with all her heart and soul. She wanted to be with him, and if the only way was to accept his terms, then she would accept them, no matter what future grief would be laid up in store for her.

You only live once, she told herself forcefully, and whatever Peter was willing to give her of his life she would take with gratitude, day by day, not looking beyond the moment. But her mind could not control the emotional turmoil churning through her body. Her legs wobbled as she took the few necessary steps to Peter's door, and her hand was shaking as it lifted to signal her surrender.

CHAPTER ELEVEN

IT was the music that stopped her. Lyn's mind had been so intensely concentrated on her decision that she had not heard it. Only in that heart-thudding moment before her knuckles made contact with Peter's door did the muted strains of an orchestra creep into her ears. She froze.

It had not occurred to her that Peter might have company. Her own need had imagined him waiting for her, available, ready to answer whenever she called. But why should he be waiting? She had gone out with Damien. Peter had held out the opportunity for her to include him in the party, and she had knocked him back. She could hardly blame him if he had then turned to another woman. But Lyn felt she would die if he had.

She leaned forward, pressing her ear to the door, compelled to settle the torment in her mind. She heard no word, nothing to suggest a conversation taking place, but her heart grew heavier as she recognised the music being played—Wagner's *Tristan and Isolde*, the most erotic love music ever composed.

A wave of nausea accompanied the thought of Peter in bed . . . making love. No, having sex. With some skilled exercise companion. Of course he would not be talking; he would be far too busy to talk. As busy as his hands had been that first morning with Jessie.

Lyn recoiled in silent anguish and dragged her feet over to her own door. Pride dictated that she could not go to him if he had turned so quickly to someone else. Yet he could not have had another woman since Lyn had moved into her apartment. He had been with her, almost every day. And night. And he had said he would wait for her.

She meant something to him—had to, or he would not have given her so much of himself. Even if he was with another woman tonight, it couldn't mean much to him. Just as Damien had not meant anything to Lyn. But if Peter was having sex ...

Lyn shook her head in tortured helplessness. She loved him. Dear God! She loved him and needed him and wanted him, and if he had turned to some other woman she had to know. Back she reeled to his door and knocked, not the carefree rat-a-tat-tat that had been their personal signal, but a wretched tattoo of hope and despair.

Her heart counted off the seconds in painful thumps. Too many seconds. He was not coming. He was busy. He did not want to be interrupted. Tears filmed Lyn's eyes as she wrenched herself away. The feet that took her across the empty hallway to her empty apartment were lumps of lead. It did no good telling herself she was a fool for loving Peter Kelso. No good at all. Blindly she pushed her key home in its lock, turned it. The door clicked open.

'Lyn!'

Music swamped the hallway, big, emotionally

binding music, pulling her round to Peter. He stood in his doorway, the red-and-black bathrobe only loosely covering his nakedness. His hair was all awry. The dark eyes stabbed across the short distance between them, taking in the signs of distress, questioning, probing. And Lyn was tremblingly aware that the tension of the moment was not wholly hers.

'Did you knock?' he asked softly.

There was a tight constriction in her throat and she had to force words past it. 'Yes. But ... the music. I thought ... you probably had company.'

He shook his head and a wry smile curved his mouth. 'I thought *you* had company, but here you've arrived home alone. And early. And upset. Damien give you a rough time?'

He was alone. Lyn's relief was so intense that she barely heard his words. And did not think to answer them. Peter was alone: that was all that mattered.

He lifted one hand in an open gesture of availability, and concern threaded his voice as he asked, 'Can I do anything for you, Lyn?'

Tears welled into her eyes again. He was so generous, so giving. Never once had he disappointed her when she had needed anything. Even now, after she had rejected him for Damien whom he despised, in front of Damien, Peter still held out his hand to her.

'Yes,' she said huskily as a wave of love swept away her doubts and fears. Her eyes questioned his, hoping against hope that she could reach his heart. 'If it's not too late, I'd like to join you.'

'It's never too late,' he said gently, bridging the awkwardness of her question with consummate ease.

'I'd ... I'd like to change out of these clothes.'

'Whatever you want.'

I want what you want, she told him silently, but she knew there was a more telling means of communication. 'I'll only be a minute. Wait for me?'

His smile curled round her heart. 'Won't move a step.'

Lyn was lightheaded with happiness as she rushed into her bedroom. Peter had waited for her. He wanted her ... maybe as much as she wanted him. She tossed off her clothes and dragged on her wrap-around housecoat. The cool silk brushed against her nakedness, awakening a sensual awareness which excited her into a trembling anticipation of Peter's touch. She hoped he would not be disappointed in her. She was so ignorant. Totally inexperienced. But surely his experience would make up for her lack of it?

With quick, slightly nervous hands, she rolled up the 'Sunrise' bedspread and hoisted it over her shoulder. Peter had said that was how he wanted her—under it, with him. She walked out to him, determined purpose in every step as she left her safe port of security, locked the door on it, and turned to the man she loved.

There were probably few times in his life that Peter Kelso registered surprise, let alone shock. This was one of them. It lasted no longer than a second, but that second changed his whole demeanour from welcome to tense restraint.

'Lyn ...' Even his voice sounded strained. His eyes searched hers with sharp urgency. 'If Damien has hurt you I'll kill the bastard, but this ... not on some emotional rebound, Lyn. When you really know your own mind.'

'I know it. Damien has nothing to do with this.' Her confidence cracked under Peter's continued appraisal. His tension sent a sickening rush of blood to her head. 'Isn't this what you've always wanted?'

'Yes, but ...'

'Have you changed your mind?'

'I've always known my own mind. And spoken it, Lyn,' he reminded her gently.

She took a deep breath to calm herself. 'Please believe me.'

He hesitated only a second longer, but it seemed the longest second of all time to Lyn. Then he stepped forward and took the bedspread from her. Her hand was trembling as he folded it into his own. There was no elation in his eyes. They swept her with a cloudy darkness. In silence he led her into his living-room and dumped the bedspread on the nearest chair.

Lyn bridled at his rough handling of it. 'You did offer fifty thousand dollars for that bedspread,' she reminded him in an attempt to lighten his mood.

'Always get your priorities right, Lyn,' he murmured as he turned to her. 'You're more important.'

He curved an arm round her shoulders and drew

her out on to the balcony. The one table lamp which had dimly lit the living-room lost all effect in the blanketing darkness of the night. The stars were silver pinpoints on black velvet.

'I love being out here. It's so beautiful,' Lyn breathed happily. Her eyes shone up at Peter. 'With you,' she added in a self-conscious whisper.

Slowly and gently he turned her into his embrace. One hand reached up and brushed her hair away from her forehead. His mouth moved round her temples, warm, tender. 'I've wanted to do this for such a long time,' he murmured. His hand slid under her chin, tilting it. There was a soft glitter in the eyes that bored into hers. 'Let the world look on. Let the angels dream.'

And the words were carried to her mouth, impressing themselves on lips which were only too ready to receive them. There was nothing tantalising in Peter's kiss, but a sweet tenderness which pierced her soul, and the urgency to give him all of herself was in her response. And yet he stopped her, withdrawing on a heavy sigh and moving her apart from him, holding her as if she was some fragile, precious thing which might break under his touch.

'I want this to be right for you, and it won't be right if you're not ready, if you're under stress, reacting to something else. Tell me what happened tonight, Lyn.'

She shook her head, evading his too perceptive gaze. 'I don't want to talk about it. Please . . .' she looked up in desperate appeal ' . . . can't you just accept me, Peter?'

His hand cupped her face with a gentleness which tightened her throat and turned the rest of her to jelly.

'Lyn, this can be traumatic for you or the loveliest experience of all. Which would you rather?'

'I want it to be good,' she choked out.

'Then your attitude's got to be right. Like anything you do, if you're reaching for the perfect result, you can't have something else distracting you.'

She looked at him helplessly, a sudden fear vibrating through her body. 'Peter, I've made up my mind and I want it to be the best for both of us, but I've had no experience at all.'

A grin slowly spread across his face, a happy, joyous grin. 'That's great! then you haven't had any wrong training.'

A nervous giggle tickled her tight throat. He was mad! Putting the whole thing in absurd terms. But then she realised that the terms were those he would naturally use. He considered sex a physical game— for which one trained. A sharp sense of deflation prompted the words, 'I wish . . .'

'What do you wish?'

I wish it was more than a game, she thought sadly, but it was no use wanting Peter on any terms but his own. And she did want him. 'I guess you're a great trainer,' she sighed.

'For you, only the best. Are you comfortable with nudity, Lyn?' he asked matter-of-factly, as if it was any everyday topic they might be discussing. 'What I mean is, are you comfortable with your own body or do you cover it up all the time?'

'I ... I can live with it,' she answered self-consciously. 'I'm not exactly built like Delvene, but I don't mind what I am.'

'Delvene ...' Peter frowned over the name as he turned her round and took her back into the living-room. Wagner's music swirled round them once more, enveloping them in its swelling emotion. 'It's not so much the body that makes for great sex, Lyn,' he assured her. 'It's the person inside ... letting go ... making it happen.'

He undid the tie-belt of her housecoat and slid it off her shoulders, lightly caressing her arms as he pushed the sleeves down until the garment dropped to the floor. And all the while his dark, knowing eyes held hers, promising her that only she, the person, mattered, and he did not care in the least what was being revealed. He took her hands and placed them on his belt.

'Now me,' he ordered softly.

Lyn's fingers were shaking so much that they fumbled over the loose knot. When his robe finally hung free, she pushed it over his broad, muscular shoulders and down his arms, copying his actions as if they were a blueprint she had to follow. It was less frightening if she didn't have to think. The bathrobe dropped to the floor. Peter grinned at her, a mad, infectious grin which somehow suggested they were terribly naughty children, but wasn't it fun? Lyn found herself grinning back.

'Dance with me,' he commanded.

It was hardly dance music. He really was mad—

hopelessly mad. But they moved their bodies to a soaring strand of music which stirred the soul, and Lyn's shaken mind caught the madness. Laughter suddenly gurgled up inside her and burst forth until her body was drawn into full contact with his. Then the laughter choked into a gasp at the sheer eroticism of their mutual nakedness.

Pinpricks of electricity shot through her entire body, forcing an intense physical awareness. The initial shock was startling enough, but as the soaring music swirled into their souls their body contacts kept changing, arousing different sensations, shocking her anew, fascinating her, exciting her, tempting her to experiment with movements of her own.

A male body was so different, hard, strong, muscular, the complete contrast to her own pliant softness. The complement, she realised, instinctively recognising the female urge to fuse with the aggressive protection of male strength, and knowing in her heart that her choice of mate would always have been Peter, no matter what the future held. She wound her arms round his neck and clung unashamedly, loving the whole feel of him against her.

'More relaxed now?' he murmured against her ear.

'Mmm.'

His hand ran down her spine, curving her closer. 'Tell me what happened, Lyn? What made you come tonight?'

She sighed and nestled her head under his ear.

She didn't mind speaking about it now. Being with Peter like this, the rest of the evening had faded into insignificance. 'You were right about Damien,' she mumbled.

'Delvene swept him off his feet.'

Lyn jerked her head back and looked up in surprise. 'How did you know that?'

'She was on your mind earlier.'

'Well, she's not any more. And she doesn't affect me any more either,' she said with satisfaction. 'You can't imagine how dull they were, Peter.'

He slanted his eyebrows in mock consideration. 'I think I might have a good idea.'

She laughed. It was good to be with him. He knew. He understood everything. Her eyes sparkled up at him. 'Know what I did?'

'Tell me.'

'I paired them off. Then when they got too much to bear I left them.'

'Revoltingly rude, 'Peter reproved her, his lips twitching in amusement.

'Abominably,' Lyn agreed with a grin. 'I simply thought about what you might do, and I did it.'

Peter grinned back. 'I knew you had a fine mind. And I love your breasts rubbing against my chest like that. Tease me with them. Be wicked. It's delicious!'

She enjoyed being deliciously wicked and felt a decidedly wicked thrill of power when Peter's arousal became all too evident. Her eyes flirted with the knowledge. 'You are awfully stimulated.'

'Awfully.' He grinned his shamelessness. 'Does it frighten you?'

'No, not now. It wasn't really because of Damien and Delvene that I came home to you, Peter.'

His eyes smiled into hers. 'I know that, Lyn. I just wanted you to know it too.'

Then the smile in his eyes flared into desire. He kissed her, and the kiss grew more and more devouring as Lyn responded with all the pent-up passion in her soul. Peter swung her legs up over his arm and carried her into his bedroom. A wild exhilaration pulsed through her veins as he tossed off the bedcovers and laid her on the pillows. He kissed her again as his hand swept over her curves, igniting an excitement which Lyn poured into her response, kissing him back with an all-consuming desire to take all he was willing to give her.

He broke away, rasping in a deep breath and smiling down at her. 'Not too quickly. Let it be for ever. Keep the moment suspended in time.'

She was glad it was dark in here, too dark for him to see her aching need for his love. She reached up to touch his face and he covered her hand with his, rubbing his cheek against her palm for a moment before guiding her hand down over his body.

'I want you to touch me like this . . . yes . . . and while you're doing that, I'm going to touch you like this.'

Her skin leapt under his hand, nerves skittering in a squirm of pleasure. She tried to excite the same response in him, wanting to give satisfaction but too inexperienced to know precisely how. A light shudder under her touch gave her a thrill of power.

'Gorgeous, isn't it?' Peter said knowingly. 'Now I'll show you how to increase the excitement, the sense of anticipation.'

And he did so with such devastating sureness that Lyn soon forgot what he wanted of her. She was totally distracted by what he was doing and it was unbelievably erotic. Her body was no longer under her control. It responded only to him, quivering, arching, twisting, melting. Her hands were clenching, mindlessly clutching at anything within reach, and her breath was pumping out in harsh sobs.

'Peter . . .' she cried, appealing for she knew not what, yet instinctively knowing that he was the master of her fate.

'Is it unbearable yet?'

Her head threshed from side to side as exquisite torture racked her body. 'Yes . . . no . . . I don't know,' she gasped.

'Soon,' he promised.

And it went on until suddenly the tension snapped and her whole body shuddered with the sweet release that rushed through her. Then Peter came to her and she accepted him with a sigh of utter fulfillment. Nothing in her whole life had ever felt so right as did that first thrust of his body entering hers, and she drew him down to her, holding him tight, owning him with all her heart and soul. He kissed her softly, soothing her ragged breathing.

'Now come with me, Lyn,' he murmured.

And it was not over. Peter drove her through

peak after peak of excitement, moving her to one position after another so that their bodies captured every nuance of touch and pleasure, and Lyn learnt an exultant abandonment to sensuality which held her in thrall. Nothing else mattered but its continuance, until she was so exhausted that she lay limp in his arms, and even then her body still sang with delight at his touch.

'Satisfied?' asked Peter, his lips teasing hers with feathery kisses.

'I think so,' she breathed on a sigh as another delicious ripple travelled through her.

'I think we should make this a fulltime occupation. There are a lot of embellishments we can use on these movements. Little subtleties we can try for more pleasure...'

'More!' A hysterical laugh gurgled out of her throat, followed by a sharp stab of desolation. Had he found her a disappointment after all his women of experience? Had all he felt was physical pleasure, no sense of oneness at all? 'I guess it's not so good with a novice,' she said flatly.

'Don't ever undervalue yourself again,' he commanded sternly. 'You're an incredible woman.' His voice dropped to a soft, whimsical note. 'I can't remember when I've ever enjoyed myself more.'

His mouth brushed hers once again and she put her arms round his neck, deepening the kiss and pressing herself against him, desperately wanting to impress herself on his heart and make him feel what she felt.

'See how incredible you are,' he groaned as he

came up for air. 'You've aroused me again.'

She laughed. He was incorrigibly mad and bad, but she loved him. She loved everything about him; the quirkiness of his clever, perceptive mind; his kind, caring humanity; and the sensual knowledge his body used so well.

His hand lightly caressed her breasts. 'You're beautiful to me, Lyn,' he said softly.

Her smile thanked him. 'I'm glad you think so.'

'I know so,' he declared, and cradled her comfortably against him. 'Now you can go to sleep and dream about the fantastic mountains we're going to climb tomorrow.'

'Mmm.'

'But if you snuggle up to me like that ...'

'Tomorrow,' she mumbled happily. And tomorrow, and tomorrow, and tomorrow, she hoped.

He sighed and nuzzled the back of her neck. 'Just as well I'm a patient man.'

Lyn thought so too. A wonderfully patient man. Delvene ... Damien ... all her past life melted into nothing compared to this night with Peter. She felt so good, as if she had lived to the full, and there could be no more that she could possibly experience that would surpass this. With a sigh of utter contentment she drifted into sleep.

CHAPTER TWELVE

A tickle on her ear raised Lyn to consciousness and a kiss on her nose awoke her completely. She looked up into Peter's smiling face; a shiny, clean-shaven face, and the scent of his after-shave lotion was sharp and tangy. She stretched, enjoying her new awareness of all her senses. 'What time is it?' she asked lazily.

'Eleven. And I can't wait any longer. You've been lying there asleep, tantalising me unbearably for the last two hours. I've brought you coffee and I'm about to cook breakfast. You've already had eight hours' rest, and there are things we have to do today that have never been done before. Let's start with toes.'

She wriggled away, laughing as she tried to escape his teasing fingers. 'That's not fair on empty toes! Breakfast, you said.'

'Bacon and eggs and lashings of toast?'

'Mmm, sounds great!'

'A woman of lusty appetites.' His grin was entirely wicked. 'I brought your housecoat in, but don't put it on. I like you the way you are.'

'You've got a robe on.'

'A small matter of temporary protection. Bacon can spit in a very nasty fashion. Don't be long.'

Lyn bounced out of bed, feeling blissfully happy.

She dashed off to the bathroom, had a quick shower, borrowed Peter's comb and toothbrush, then, tingling with anticipation, she presented herself in the kitchen.

Breakfast was fun. Peter insisted they should sit at the dining-table as for a formal meal, and there they sat in their nakedness, facing each other down the length of the table. Lyn giggled at the absurdity of it, but never had she enjoyed a meal so much. The food was delicious, but the look in Peter's eyes was even more delicious. It was possessive.

'Why do you enchant me so much?' he mused, and for once his expression was serious.

Before Lyn could think of an answer, a knock on the door jarred her thoughts. Peter's gaze did not shift at all. It was fixed on her.

'Aren't you going to answer it?' she asked in a flutter of uncertainty.

He smiled. 'Today, as far as the rest of the world is concerned, I'm officially dead.'

She felt a warm satisfaction. He wanted no one but her. 'Were you expecting someone?'

'No one.'

The knock came again, sharp and impatient.

'You'd better answer it.'

Peter sighed. 'Only to please you.'

He pushed back his chair and stood up. Lyn admired his superb physique as he shrugged on his bathrobe and belted it carelessly. She no longer cared how many women had shared his bed. Right now he was hers, all hers. And whoever was outside would be sent away. The knock came again, and

Peter interrupted it as he opened the door.

'Good morning,' he said breezily. 'Or is it afternoon?'

'Mr Kelso . . .'

Lyn's heart catapulted around her chest. It was her mother's voice. Her prune voice which was invariably used for tight disapproval.

'I apologise for interrupting your . . . your . . .'

'Breakfast,' Peter supplied helpfully.

Lyn could imagine all too clearly what was running through her mother's mind at the sight of Peter's loosely tied bathrobe. At the sight of her daughter's nakedness she would probably have a fit. Thank God Peter would send her away.

'I'm Alicia Mansfield, Lynette's mother.'

'Of course you are. Henrietta told me all about you, Alicia. Pleased to meet you at last.'

Lyn almost choked. Her mother's haughty dignity would be shot to pieces by Peter's irreverent manner.

'Mr Kelso . . .' Pure frost.

'Please call me Peter. For all practical purposes I feel like one of the family.'

'Mr Kelso . . .' absolute ice. 'I have been trying to get in touch with my daughter Lynette all morning. She's not at home and . . .'

'Quite right! She's at home with me, having breakfast. As a matter of fact we were about to finish off with a cup of coffee. Like to join us? Have a bit of chit-chat before we get down to the serious things of life?'

Lyn almost died on the spot. A burst of adrenalin

sent her flying into the bedroom for her housecoat.
How could Peter be so indiscreet? So—outrageous,
she acknowledged with a sinking heart.

'Lynette ... is with you?' Strangled shock.

There was nothing for it but to brazen out the
situation if her mother came in, Lyn thought,
sliding back into her seat at the table. This was the
life she wanted. With Peter. Her mother would only
have come to castigate her about her behaviour last
night. Delvene would have painted the worst
possible picture.

'Of course she's with me. Where else would she
be?' Peter frowned as if Lyn's mother was singularly
slow not to have figured that out. 'Come now,
Alicia. She's perfectly safe.'

'Safe!' A squawk of scorn.

'Wouldn't hurt her for the world,' Peter declared
blithely. 'Are you coming in or not, Alicia? It isn't
really seemly for me to be entertaining you at the
door in my bathrobe. Though come to think of it,
Lyn might prefer to entertain you in hers.' He poked
his head round the door and grinned at her. 'Ah, I
see you've got dressed. You really shouldn't feel shy
with your mother, you know. After all, she did give
birth to you.'

'I'm coming in.' Said in the tone of one
determined to take the bull by the horns.

'And very welcome you are too,' burbled Peter
opening the door wide.

Lyn tensed, even while telling herself that he was
right and there was no cause for shame or
embarrassment. But she didn't want to hurt her

mother, or even offend her. Alicia Mansfield marched in, coming to an abrupt halt as her outraged gaze found Lyn seated at the table.

Lyn tried a peacemaking smile. 'Hello, Mother.'

The outraged gaze grew more outraged as it swept over the silk housecoat, taking in the evidence that only nudity existed beneath it. 'So! It's come to this! You've let this man corrupt you.'

Rebellion stirred. Why was she always wrong in everything she did? Why always the judgement without even considering Lyn's viewpoint? 'I don't think so, Mother,' she said slowly. 'I did have some say in it. Actually, Peter has taught me a lot of good things and I'm very grateful to him.'

The reply visibly shook her mother. Then disapproval became even more bitterly set.

'Lyn, how many times do I have to tell you I don't want your gratitude?' Peter put in with a pained expression. 'What will your mother think if you talk of gratitude? Though I must say, Alicia, I'm grateful to you for producing such a marvellous woman as this daughter of yours. By God, Gerald must be a happy man having you as his wife! Please make yourself at home with us.' He held out a chair, inviting her to sit at the table with them.

Alicia Mansfield stared at him as if he was mad. She shook her head slightly and returned dazed eyes to Lyn. 'He's turned your mind, Lynette,' she said accusingly. 'I couldn't believe Delvene this morning when she told me what you did last night. You weren't brought up to behave so rudely. But I can believe it now. I can believe anything!'

Had there really been any doubt? Lyn wondered cynically. Hadn't her parents always believed what Delvene told them? Not that it mattered now. Only Peter mattered. Any reply to her mother was futile. She held her tongue.

'Splendid?' said Peter. 'Terrible having a closed mind, Alicia. You really should open it to all experiences of life. Now do sit down. I'll get you a cup of coffee. How do you like it?'

'I don't want your coffee,' she snapped. 'I want to talk to my daughter. If you don't mind.'

'Not at all. Lyn, your mother wants to talk to you. But before you start, Alicia, let me advise you that I won't tolerate any reference to what Delvene says or does. Lyn has suffered quite enough on that score. As far as I can see Delvene has had all your attention and all your affection and everything she could take from Lyn besides. Even Lyn's men. Instead of indulging Delvene, if you and her father had disciplined that greedy, selfish streak in her from childhood onwards, she wouldn't need a spanking now. I nearly did it for you the day she came to seduce me.'

Lyn's choked gasp brought an instant switch of attention from Alicia's shocked face. Peter's smile was one of limpid innocence. 'I'm afraid that's true, Lyn. Delvene doesn't understand faithfulness. She wasn't at all pleased when I told her you weren't yet finished with me. She said some very rude things. I sent her off, suitably chastened by a few choice words of my own.'

He turned back to her mother. 'Delvene might

look grown up, Alicia, but she's just a spoilt, wilful child who's clever enough to clothe herself in sweet innocence. You and Gerald have some work ahead of you there. She needs to be looked after very carefully. And you should start now.'

A touch of steel crept into his tone as he continued. 'Now, if you want to talk to Lyn, please do so, but keep in mind that you're speaking to a daughter you've almost lost through your disapproval and negligence. And if you're not very careful, Alicia, you'll lose her altogether, for I will not stand by and hear her unjustly maligned by you or anyone.'

It was too much for Alicia Mansfield. She couldn't cope with Peter at all. She was shocked, bewildered, and so shaken up that even her face seemed to wobble as she turned to Lyn. Tears of confusion welled up in her eyes. 'Lynette ... this isn't right for you. I can't pretend that I ever really understood you, and I never knew how to deal with you. You were always so withdrawn, so intense. But you are my daughter and I do love you, and I only want the best for you. This man can only bring you grief.'

She glanced fearfully at Peter before rushing on. 'I didn't want you to leave home, Lynette. You know I didn't. And your father ... he's ... he's still upset about your going. Please come back with me.'

Did they want her? Did they love her? Had she put the distance between herself and her parents, making it difficult for them to express their love?

But she had tried so hard, and her mother had not come today with love on her mind.

Lyn dragged in a deep breath and shook her head. 'I don't want to leave here, Mother. I'm sorry you don't understand, but for me, this is the best. I know it must be terribly hard for you to accept, and please believe I'm not doing this to hurt you or Father. More than anything else, I want to be with Peter, and as long as he wants me, I'll stay with him.'

'Lynette . . .' Alicia could not go on. Tears were rolling down her cheeks and she shook her head in mute distress.

Lyn rose to her feet, instinctively wanting to comfort, but the urge was strangled by years of inhibitions. Delvene was the daughter who hugged and kissed. Lyn had been unable to compete with her sister for her parents' affection, and she couldn't bring herself to take the step now. Her hands lifted in an awkward gesture of helplessness. 'Mother . . . please . . . don't cry. It is all right—truly.'

'How can it be right?' Her mother choked out and drew in a ragged breath. Her eyes stabbed a pained accusation at her. 'And you know it's your father's fiftieth birthday next week. The invitations for the party went out before you left home. He's counting on your coming. And all our friends will be there. It won't be right at all if you're not with us.'

Lyn's heart steeled. It was the same old painful story. All her mother was worrying about was what her friends would say. Lyn was finished with that life. However, before she could form a reply Peter took over.

'Wouldn't dream of missing such an important family occasion,' he beamed, stepping over to lay a hand on Lyn's shoulder in the age-old gesture of partnership. 'Not to worry, Alicia, we'll certainly be there.'

'You!' It was a strangled gasp of horror.

Lyn herself was stunned by Peter's move. The hand on her shoulder gently kneaded her soft flesh, transmitting a message of comforting reassurance.

'Been looking forward to meeting Gerald for a long time,' he continued blithely. 'Very astute man, your husband—subscribes to my newsletter. Yes, I can see this is going to be the social event of the year. And I haven't seen Max for a while either. It'll be a great night. I assume you've invited Madeleine?'

The horror had frozen into a daze. 'Madeleine?'

'Madeleine Kane. She and her husband are great friends of mine. Don't worry, I'll invite them myself. No social occasion could be called an occasion without Madeleine to cover it. Lyn's father deserves the best. One should always go straight to the top, Alicia.'

Lyn had to bite her lips to prevent a smile. Peter was fighting her mother's snobbery with snobbery and turning her world upside down. Usually Deborah King, the society journalist, covered her mother's parties. Alicia was absolutely dumbstruck that Peter could call on the editor of the whole newspaper.

She was obviously in a terrible quandry. On the one hand she recoiled from the thought of Peter's being a guest, particularly as Lyn's escort, but on the other hand, Madeleine Kane's presence would be a social coup, not to mention the presence of her husband, Max Abrams, an entrepreneur of international standing.

Before she could come to grips with the situation, Peter had moved, taking her arm and steering her towards the door. 'Now don't you worry about a thing, Alicia. Lyn and I will turn up in grand style, Madeleine will give the party a marvellous write-up, and Gerald will be pleased about everything. How could he not be when he has such a wonderful wife?' He opened the door and ushered her out. 'Lovely to have met you. You must come and visit us as often as you like—Lyn and I are at home most of the time. Just give us a call. 'Bye now.'

There was not a word from Alicia. Lyn imagined the helpless look of perplexity on her mother's face. Aunt Henrietta had been right: Peter was a genius and a fool, and the mixture was a heady brew that left most people punch-drunk.

Having closed the door, he turned back to Lyn with an oddly grim look of satisfaction on his face. 'A very receptive woman, your mother. By the time I've finished with her, she'll take on a new view of life. As will your father. To whom I intend to speak when we meet.'

Lyn shook her head at him in helpless bemusement. No doubt her father would end up punch-drunk too. 'You won't hurt them, Peter? I don't want them to be hurt.'

He shook his head. 'I'll only be doing them a kindness, I promise.' His face softened in concern as he slid his arms round her waist and drew her close. 'You weren't in too much distress with your mother, were you, Lyn?.'

'Not too much,' she agreed, leaning against him and holding him tight. She breathed a sigh of contentment. Of course he was quite mad, but it was a madness she loved, and she had ceased to think him the least bit bad, or dangerous. 'I'm just fine with you,' she murmured.

'Good!' He kissed her forehead. 'I'd hate to think ...' he kissed her nose ' ... you weren't fit enough ...' he brushed her lips with his ' ... to come mountain-climbing with me.'

Then he kissed her with a passion that was as inspirational as any mountain which might present itself, and Lyn was only too happy to follow his lead. Anywhere. Any time.

CHAPTER THIRTEEN

LYN sighed and dropped her hand on the dressing-table. She drew in several slow, deep breaths and willed her fingers to stop trembling. Tonight of all nights she did not want to make a mess of her eye make-up. Peter had gone to so much trouble and expense. He had called in the best couturier in Sydney to make the dress he wanted her to wear. The least she could do was try to look her very best for him. But no matter how much she argued with herself, she could not quell the sick apprehension in her stomach.

She loved Peter with all her heart and there was nothing she would not do for him, but she had been a Mansfield too long to shrug off completely the family's feeling, their pride and their high sense of propriety. She was Peter Kelso's mistress, and if the fact was not immediately obvious to her parents' friends, Peter would surely say something which would leave them in no doubt. She did not mind for herself, but her parents would feel it deeply, and for all their shortcomings as parents, she took no pleasure in hurting them.

Nevertheless, there had been no way to back out of the situation. Peter was all too intent on going, and she would not deny him. Her father had telephoned, insisting that he wanted her to come to his party, and if that meant her bringing Peter Kelso, then he would be pleased to meet the man. And talk with him.

Lyn could well imagine the kind of talk her father would wish to have with Peter, but there was no doubt in her mind who would end up feeling chastened. It would never be Peter. Only God knew how the evening would end. She just hoped Peter would curb his outrageousness a little and not ruin the party for her father. Or her mother. After all, it was their home and their friends and their life. Lyn was content to let them be if they simply refrained from criticising her.

She concentrated hard on keeping her hand steady, and completed her make-up to her satisfaction. In fact, she was really pleased with her mirrored self. She looked good. Better than good. The new hairstyle which Peter had personally supervised was very flattering and feminine with its wispy curls feathering a soft frame for her face.

'Admiring yourself?' Peter teased as he came into the bedroom. He leaned over and placed a large velvet box on the dressing-table, then kissed the nape of her neck before straightening up. 'I'm glad I'm in time to help you dress. Of course, undressing you usually gives me more pleasure, but tonight . . .' His hands caressed her shoulders as he smiled at her in the mirror. There was a strange gleam of excitement in his eyes, of almost triumphant anticipation. 'Tonight you will be dressed as befits you, and the cream of Sydney society will look on and gasp in envy and admiration.'

She laughed and shook her head, unable to imagine that ever happening, but enormously pleased that Peter should think it possible. As long as he thought her beautiful, Lyn was perfectly happy as she was.

'First the dress,' Peter said with the eagerness of an impresario, and turned to lift it off the bed.

It was a fabulous dress, virtually a period costume since it had been copied from an old, old photograph. Lyn had privately put Peter's insistence on it in the realm of eccentricity, but eccentric or not, the finished creation was stunning. The style had been slightly modernised in so far as it did not have a bustle, but the old-world elegance had been retained in its intricate tucks and folds and graceful drapery.

Peter held it out for her to step into, and Lyn needed no further urging. The black silk taffeta rustled as she slid her arms into the sleeves. He fitted the bodice to her curves, taking and giving sensual delight as he did so, then deftly but slowly fastened the long row of covered buttons up her back. The dress had been made to fit her like a second skin, and its dark richness flattered her figure.

Indeed, it was the most beautiful, most exciting, most incredible gown she had ever seen, let alone worn. She stared at her reflection, realising that her new hairdo was right for the old-fashioned style, and silently acknowledging that Peter had known what he was about. As always.

'And now for the finishing touch,' he said with relish.

The velvet box was clicked open and from it he lifted a necklace which Lyn instantly recognised. It was the same as that worn by the woman in the photograph. The photograph from which the dress had been copied.

'Peter ...'

She swallowed hard as he laid it reverently round her neck and fastened it with a decisive click. Her hand lifted and nervously fingered the ornate design, panels of gold, finely chained together and encrusted with rubies and pearls. They were real gems, Lyn knew it with absolute certainty ... the brilliance of the stones, the fine lustre of the pearls ... and Peter would never have anything to do with fakes. But if they were real, this necklace must be worth an absolute fortune.

'Perfect,' he breathed as his eyes swept her reflection.

'Peter, I ... I can't wear this,' Lyn got out huskily.

'Why not? The dress and jewellery were made for each other. You see? The perfect complements.'

'But ... but they're real, aren't they?'

He laughed, a pure bubble of elation as he leaned over and gathered up the pendant earrings from the box. 'There are two security guards outside who surely believe it! I'm afraid your parents will have to put up with them hanging around the house tonight. The insurance company insisted. Here, put these on, I want to see the whole effect.'

The temptation to see them on herself was too great to resist, yet as she obeyed him Lyn kept wondering if she should be refusing. Then her reflection was so fascinating that she gave up worrying. She simply stared. The woman in the mirror was not Lyn Mansfield; it was someone from a world of past opulence, brought glowingly to life. She remembered Damien's sneering at Peter's taste for opulence, but no one could ever sneer at this. It was the marvellous opulence of fairy tales, of kings and queens and myths and legends.

'Where did you get such jewellery?' she asked in an awed whisper.

'It was made for the Hohenzollerns, a ruling family in Europe for over nine hundred years. The woman in the photograph you saw was the Princess Marie-Thérèse. She wore the dress and the jewellery at the last reception before the abdication in 1918.'

Heavens! He had dressed her as a princess, Lyn thought in incredulous wonder.

'The jewellery disappeared for many years,' Peter rambled on. 'It surfaced in Argentina some twenty years after the Second World War. As you know, I have a passion for unique things, and I couldn't resist buying it.'

'So it's yours?' she gasped.

The dark eyes glowed at her for a long moment before the smile came. It was slow, gathering a rich pleasure that sent a strange tingle through Lyn's entire body.

'It's yours, Lyn,' he said softly.

'No, no, I can't accept it,' she babbled frantically. 'A fortune! It must be worth a fortune.'

'It suits you. Just as I knew it would.'

'It doesn't suit me at all. How can you say that?'

He just grinned at her, and of course the reflection in the mirror mocked her claim.

She heaved a fluttery sigh. 'All right, I'll wear it tonight because you want me to, but I can't possibly keep it.'

'You will,' he said with his supreme confidence. 'Tonight you'll be the toast of the town, and there'll be no prouder parents than yours. Now let me show you off to Max and Madeleine. I've left them in the living-room with a bottle of champagne.'

Show her off. Now she understood. Peter's perception was masterly, as usual. Dressed as she was, Lyn was automatically lifted beyond criticism in any social circle. And to top it off, she and Peter would arrive at the party with Madeleine Kane and Max Abrams, personalities who were welcome everywhere. She hugged Peter's arm in an excess of gratitude. He had thought of everything and was indeed a genius.

'Happy now?'

'Yes, thank you. Only you could have done this.'

'Ah, but only you could have made it possible.'

The softly spoken remark gave Lyn a wonderful glow of confidence as Peter ushered her into his living-room.

'My God!'

Madeleine Kane's mouth stayed open as her gaze swept over Lyn and glued itself to the necklace. She rose from her chair as if drawn by a magnet. She was a tall, thin woman, made taller by the highly piled red hair, and was quite a stunning picture herself in a bright lime-green gown. Peter performed the introductions as she zeroed in on Lyn.

'I've never seen anyone look so magnificent! When you promise, Peter, you certainly deliver,' Madeleine declared with arch satisfaction. 'I'd give up my eye-teeth, and the story, to wear that jewellery, Lyn.'

Max ambled up behind his wife. 'And a fair bit more,' he teased with a smile at Lyn.

He was a handsome man with a very polished look about him. The grey amongst his curly black hair suggested he was a few years older than Peter, but the twinkling brown eyes indicated that he shared the same zest for life and all its pleasures.

'Personally, I'd rather have the "Sunrise" bedspread,' he drawled. 'I've got to have one of your creations, Lyn. Peter says you'll design one especially for our room. Just call us when you're free. Any time at all. Any price.'

Lyn beamed, absolutely elated by their compliments. 'I'd be happy to do that, Max. Thank you.'

'Good! And might I say you've just made my night worthwhile. I must confess these society dos are more Maddie's cup of tea than mine, but Peter always seems to conjure up something special.'

Peter chuckled. 'I did tell you Lyn was special, Max.'

'Ah, but you have a talent for the totally unexpected. And the very beautiful.'

Peter's chuckle became a full-throated laugh. 'And the night has just begun, my friend. Let's be off.'

As they rode down in the lift Max chivvied his friend on the inconvenience. 'Damned if I know why you don't get yourself a decent house, Peter.'

'I tried it once. It's not for me ... servant problems, maintenance problems, security problems, people taking up your time. You can have them, Max. Up here I'm as free as a bird. Can come and go as I please without a care in the world.'

'How do you like it, Lyn?' Madeleine asked curiously. 'You've lived in a mansion with servants all your life, haven't you?'

'And hated it. I'm with Peter,' she replied firmly, covering the momentary pang she had felt at Peter's declaration of freedom. She might be with Peter, but she couldn't imagine that he would ever accept any ties ... not the tie she wanted most of all. But what more could a woman ask than what Peter had given her? Lyn hugged that thought to herself and was content.

They drove to the Mansfield mansion in Max's white Rolls Royce, with Madeleine extracting all the details about Lyn's dress and jewellery along the way. Once there it was Lyn who took the lead, and she was conscious of a heady anticipation as she moved them all through the arched foyer to where her parents were stationed at the entrance to the large reception room. Surely they would at least approve of her appearance tonight?

Alicia Mansfield turned from greeting the previous arrivals. The gracious welcome which had been set on her face suddenly stiffened with shock. Her eyes took on a glazed look. It seemed to Lyn that for a moment her mother had not even recognised her.

'Hello, Mother. You know Peter, of course. And this is Madeleine Kane and Max Abrams. My mother, Alicia Mansfield.'

'Lynette!' The name was a gasp of wonderment.

'Doesn't she look superb?' Madeleine tripped out on an amused laugh. 'I must congratulate you, Alicia. It must make you very proud to have two so very beautiful daughters.'

'One of whom, at least, has a very extraordinary talent,' Max added smoothly.

Lyn could not help smiling.

'Yes ... thank you, thank you,' Alicia said weakly, the society hostess struggling to recover an appropriate composure. 'It's very kind of you to come at such short notice. And we're very, very pleased to welcome you.'

Madeleine smiled broadly. 'Our pleasure. Whenever Peter calls, we know it's for something special, don't we, Max?'

He grinned at Peter. 'Should have been a showman.'

'All the world's a stage,' Peter retorted, shrugging, then smiled at Lyn's mother. 'You look lovely tonight, Alicia.'

Peter himself looked every inch the distinguished gentleman in his formal dinner suit, and his special aura of absolute assurance was even more pronounced.

Alicia's gaze flickered with uncertainty and not a little awe. 'Thank you ... Peter.' Then her gaze returned to Lyn. She shook her head a little as her eyes filmed with tears. 'You look so happy, Lynette. I wish . . . I hope you'll always be as happy.'

The wish was so obviously genuine that Lyn felt tears prick at her own eyes. She had been wrong. Her mother did love her; she really did. No matter how ineffective the love was, it was there. Impulsively Lyn leaned forward and pressed her cheek to her mother's. 'Thank you,' she whispered huskily.

'Lynette? Is it you?'

The incredulous note in Gerald Mansfield's call drew their attention. Lyn turned to greet her father as he made his return from a group of guests.

'Lyn . . .' He took her hands in his. His eyes drank her in, their expression a strange mixture of pleasure and pain. His voice, when he spoke, held a soft note of wistfulness. 'You should have always looked like this. I'm so very glad you came, my dear.'

He kept one of her hands tightly in his as he offered his free one to Peter. 'Mr Kelso, I've looked forward to meeting you. I hope before this evening's over we can find time to talk together.'

'One of the pleasures I've been anticipating all day, Gerald. And please call me Peter.' His smile was genial and inviting. 'Whenever you have a free moment, I'll be available. And now, may I introduce my friends, Madeleine Kane and Max Abrams?'

Gerald Mansfield handled the meetings with all the dignified charm of his heritage. He ushered the party into the room and ignored the buzz which went round the guests as Lyn and Peter made their entrance. Only when he had made many introductions and a convivial group had formed round the newcomers did he take his leave to return to his reception duties.

The reaction to Peter was twofold. The women regarded him with frank curiosity; the men were only too eager to engage him in conversation. There were respect and interest in his opinions as he tossed off blithe generalities, including Lyn in everything he said. Madeleine and Max were masters at the art of mixing, friendly, witty, oozing with easy charm.

But it was Lyn who was the star of the party, the focus of all eyes. Madeleine repeated the story of the dress and necklace, and the fascination of Lyn's appearance was further heightened. People stared, whispered, and stared again in admiration or envy, just as Peter had predicted.

There was only one person who pointedly ignored her, and that was Delvene. Lyn saw her sister circulating among the guests, but always at a distance. Once Lyn caught her staring at her necklace, the perfect mouth in a sulky pout, the green eyes glittering with envy.

She wondered if Delvene was too wary of Peter's tongue to risk an approach. Or perhaps Peter's lecture to her mother had borne some fruit and Delvene had been ordered to keep her distance. Whatever the reason, Lyn could not help enjoying the fact that it was she who was doing the shining tonight instead of Delvene.

Lyn was dancing with Max when she saw her father appear at Peter's side. After a short exchange of words they left the ballroom together. Heading for the library, Lyn surmised. She heaved a resigned little sigh, and hoped her father would not be too discomfited by Peter's brand of chitchat.

The dance ended. The orchestra took a break. Lyn had downed two drinks, and still Peter had not returned to her side. Nor was there any sign of her father. She began to feel edgy. She disliked not knowing what was happening. Surely they had had enough time to reach some kind of understanding? The party was not the same without Peter. All the admiration was meaningless, and she felt flat and bereft. Her mind was made up. With quick, decisive steps she walked out to the library.

It was only when she reached the heavy panelled door that she hesitated. Practically all the miseries of her life had been associated with her father's library. She hated the room. Even now, knowing that Peter was inside, she was reluctant to enter. But she made herself knock and walk right in.

Cigars! There were Peter and her father, sitting at ease in the huge leather chairs, smoking cigars. As if they were celebrating a birth. The birth of a friendship? A wry little smile tugged at her mouth as the two men rose to their feet. For years and years Lyn had tried to reach her father, never succeeding. Peter had apparently done it in a matter of minutes.

'Were you getting worried?' he asked, holding out his arm to her and drawing her to his side.

'You seemed to be gone a long time,' she answered warily.

He smiled down at her, assuring her that everything was fine. 'Your father and I had much to talk about.'

Gerald cleared his throat and spoke with a distinct note of deference. 'Peter, I appreciate that you'd like to be alone with Lynette, but I may not get another chance tonight and I very much want a few private words with my daughter. Would you mind?'

Lyn sensed his hesitation. 'It's all right, Peter.'

His smile held an ironic twist. 'I'll wait outside. Just remember that even a master of the game can always run into an unexpected hitch.'

She frowned after his departing figure, wondering what manipulative moves he had played in here with her father, who apparently understood his comment. It did seem extraordinary that there had been no tension between the two men when she had entered the room. But then, Peter was so extraordinary.

'You must love him very much, Lynette,' her father said softly.

She turned to him, a little startled at hearing her feeling put into words. She had never spoken it out loud. 'Yes, I do, Father,' she admitted quietly. 'He's . . . he's everything to me,' she added in a placatory tone, knowing that her father could not at heart approve of her living with Peter without benefit of marriage, no matter what face Peter had put upon it.

He nodded gravely. 'It had to be so. For a little while, after your mother told me you were with him, I believed it was because we'd failed you. But ...' he shook his head, 'that didn't ring true. You have a strong character. Like Henrietta. However, I know now that we did fail you in other ways, Lynette, very badly. I hope you can find it in your heart to forgive us.'

His sincerity was beyond question, and when he held out his arms to her Lyn rushed into them, hugging her father with all the pent-up feeling she had hidden from him over the years. He gently laid his cheek on her hair and patted her back in awkward affection.

'It seems a terrible indictment on my perception that I had to lose a daughter before I could really see her.' He gently pulled out of her embrace enough to look down at her face, and his eyes held a shadow of pain. 'I've been to Sinclair's showroom. Why didn't you ever show me what you could do, Lynette?'

'You didn't like me doing art, Father. You ... you always showed disapproval.'

He heaved a sigh. 'I was a stupid, blind fool. Henrietta was so right, I should have listened to her. But I am interested now, Lynette, and I'm very, very proud of you. More than that. I love all that you are, but I expect it's come too late. Peter will claim all your time, but spare a little for us, will you? Let us come and visit you?'

'You'll be very welcome, Father,' she promised him, amazed that he had changed his position so far.

He smiled his relief. 'Your Peter is quite an extraordinary fellow, you know. Quite extraordinary. He taught me what I've missed out on with you.' His gaze dropped to her necklace and he gave a little shake of his head. 'And despite his reputation, I can't doubt that he loves you very deeply.'

Love! Lyn's heart performed an uncoordinated jig.

Her father drew in a long breath. 'The last thing I expected was his asking for your hand in marriage . . .'

Marriage! Her heart stopped dead.

' . . . but considering the way he's looked after you, dressed you, even chided your parents for your sake, I feel sure he'll cherish you, Lynette. For ever. And you've chosen him. That's more than enough for me. I've been so wrong, so terribly wrong. I wish you every happiness together.' He tenderly kissed her forehead and smiled indulgently at her. 'I'll go now and send him in to you.'

Lyn's heart had pumped into life again, wild, chaotic life. Her mind jagged around her father's words, hoping, disbelieving, and finally, painfully, understanding. It was a game, the play of the unexpected. A manipulation of her father's need for respectability. A marriage which would never take place. The hitch in the game. Peter had warned her. But the disappointment was so intense that Lyn could not stop the rush of tears to her eyes.

The library door was opened. Her father walked out, and Peter walked in. This damned, damned library, Lyn thought despairingly. In instinctive defence, she turned her back on Peter, battling to stem the tears. It was an impossible task; they kept coming.

'Lyn?' Peter's voice, soft, caring, concerned.

Logic warred with emotion, but emotion was far too strong to be repelled. She swung on him, the tear-filled eyes luminous with pain. 'You didn't have to use that, Peter. The idea of marriage might be a game to you, but ... It's one thing to make Charles Sinclair jump through hoops, it's quite another to do it to my father. He believed you, Peter. It's so hurtful, to him and to me. I never thought you'd tell a lie, not even in a game. It's so ... so ...'

The look of searing intensity in his eyes made her tongue falter. 'You think this is a game?' His voice was furry with emotion.

'What ... what else can it be?'

'The game is over, Lyn. It's been over for a long, long time. I need you more than any man has ever wanted any woman.' His hands took gentle hold of her upper arms, and in his eyes was the look of love, an urgent, possessive love, without the slightest spark of amusement lurking anywhere.

'You're more precious to me than anything in the world. Incomparable. My life is worthless without you. Tonight I wanted to sweep you off your feet, and I'd planned this moment as an answer to all the romance in your soul. I hoped your father wouldn't pre-empt me in his talk with you, and I'm sorry he has. Will you marry me, my love, and share your life with me?'

Lyn stared at him disbelievingly, even while seeing the truth in his eyes and hearing the wonderful words he spoke. 'You really want to marry me?' she whispered, almost afraid to accept what she saw and heard. It meant too much.

'I most certainly do. Haven't I always known my own mind?' Peter took something from his pocket, lifted her left hand, and slowly slid on to her third finger a ring of gold, encrusted with rubies and pearls. 'Does this make it more believable, Lyn? You'll wear this . . . for me?'

'Peter . . .' She was too choked with emotion to go on, but her feeling for him shone from her eyes with telling eloquence.

He drew her into his arms and she wrapped her own arms round him, hugging him fiercely to her.

'I love you,' she said with intense passion, then leaned back to look up at him. 'I came to you with my bedspread because I loved you, Peter, and wanted to be with you always.'

'It was the only time in my life I ever felt doubt. I wasn't sure why you were doing it or what I should do. But I wanted you so much . . .' He smiled a beautiful smile. 'Thank you for giving me the most marvellous moments in my life.'

'Oh, Peter, you're so marvellous to me. And wanting to marry me . . . I'm so happy . . .'

She reached up to kiss him, and he responded with a passion which expressed all the love there could ever be between a man and a woman at such a moment of intimate revelation.

Curiosity also required satisfaction. 'When did you start to love me, Peter?' Lyn asked somewhat breathlessly when their mouths parted for a moment.

'It took a long time. About fifteen minutes after we met.'

Laughter bubbled up in her, and she laid her head against his shoulder and gave in to it until tears rolled down her cheeks. He was still mad, gloriously, wonderfully mad. And she adored his madness.

It was some considerable time later when she suggested that maybe they should rejoin the party. Peter agreed, commenting that the library was not quite the place he had in mind for what he wanted to do, and really, her father should refurnish with more consideration for others. He would speak to him about it.

The party had reached the convivial stage where speeches were being called upon. Gerald Mansfield took the stage. He was a noted public speaker at company dinners, and all the guests wore smiles of anticipation as he cleared his throat. Lyn snuggled against Peter and his arm tightened around her. She felt deliriously happy.

'It is a very pleasant thing indeed, to be surrounded by one's family and friends on such a night as this,' her father rolled out in his rich, speaking tone. 'I thank you all for being here. This party was conceived as a celebration for my having made it through a half-century of years. And I'm glad I did make it ...'

A burst of applause and affectionate laughter made him pause a few moments.

'Fifty years. A watermark, one might say. A time to look back and take stock of what one has done with one's life. I've had some great moments of happiness—unforgettable. The birth of my daughters were two of them. But I think my greatest moment of happiness came when Alicia accepted my proposal of marriage. She was, and is, and always will be, the wife of my heart.'

Another burst of applause interrupted him and Gerald smiled at Alicia, who stood nearby. Then he held up his hand for silence.

'Tonight I've been forcefully reminded of the feeling we shared when we pledged our troth, and I have great pleasure in announcing the engagement of my daughter, Lynette, to a man she loves and whose love for her is surely obvious to everyone here. He has left me in no doubt that he will cherish her as a father would want his daughter cherished. Always. Peter Kelso.'

There were gasps and stares of surprise. Madeleine gave a little shriek of delight, and it was Max who set off the somewhat belated applause, clapping loudly as he followed Madeleine in her rush to congratulate Lyn and Peter.

'I should have known. You devil, Peter! I should have known this was what you'd planned,' Madeleine cried, hugging them both with glee.

'A showman,' Max chuckled behind her.

Alicia descended upon them, kissing them both and babbling happy words of well-wishing. Lyn hugged her, blissfully free of all the inhibitions of the past. Even Delvene came forward to mouth the token congratulations, and stiffened in surprise as Lyn kissed her with a heart too full of love to hold any resentment against her sister. Delvene hesitated, then with an odd mixture of expressions on her beautiful face she leaned forward and kissed Lyn back.

'No grudges ... Lyn?' she whispered.

'None at all,' Lyn smiled, ' ... Delvene.'

'Peter!' Gerald called, inviting him to speak.

'Madeleine, this is for print,' Peter commanded before steering Lyn over to where her father stood.

An instant hush dropped over the guests, interest heightened and curiosity piqued by what they perceived as an amazing match.

'I'd like to thank Gerald for his generous support, Alicia for her graciousness. Most of you here know of me. A few of you know me. All of you have been surprised by this anouncement. But believe me, your surprise is nothing to the surprise I felt on meeting Lyn and getting to know her. Up until the very recent past, I've viewed life as a game, one I played to the full, trying out everything it offered, always searching for the ultimate, the one unique, wonderful experience which would fulfil that part of me that always remained unsatisfied. I didn't know what it was ... but now I do.'

He turned to Lyn, his eyes glowing with the richest satisfaction of all. 'Those of you who have known real love ...' he reached for her ' ... will know what Lyn and I feel now.' He gathered her into his arms. 'And you'll know why we're leaving now . . .' He kissed her, then smiled round at the crowd of bemused guests. 'We have a lot to talk about. We'll be happy to see you all at the wedding. Until then we're officially dead, so don't ring or call.' He gave a blithe wave of farewell as he swept Lyn towards the door. 'Thank you for sharing this wonderful evening with us, and a very good night to you all.'

Lyn began to laugh in the foyer and almost stumbled down the front steps in her hilarity. 'You were dreadful, Peter! Mother will probably be having a fit.'

'Not at all. She's beginning to like me, and what other hostess can boast of such a happening at her party? Besides, I simply thought of what you would do in the same situation and did it,' he retorted glibly.

'You're right,' Lyn spluttered between giggles. 'We do share something special.'

'Soulmates,' Peter breathed as he kissed her breathless.

Hand in hand they wandered down the driveway, lost to everything but their joy in each other, until Lyn caught sight of two figures trailing after them.

'Peter, we're being followed,' she whispered.

He glanced around. 'Oh hell! The security guards. That's the problem with possessions, Lyn. We'll have to get rid of that jewellery.'

'Over my dead body!'

He grinned. 'Over your body any time.' Then he turned towards the two men. 'Go and get your car.

You can give us a lift home. But no watching in the driving mirror!'

'Yes, sir. Thank you, sir. Our pleasure, sir,' came the cheery reply.

Peter's eyes sparkled down at Lyn. 'What does he know of pleasure?'

'I don't know, but you're certainly the master of it,' Lyn declared.

And it was a divine madness that swirled around them. The world could look on and wonder as much as it liked. The angels in heaven could look on and dream. For the magic they shared was indeed unique. It was immortal.

EMMA DARCY nearly became an actress until her fiancé declared he preferred to attend the theatre *with* her. She became a wife and mother. Later she took up oil painting—unsuccessfully, she remarks. Then, she tried architecture, designing the family home in New South Wales. Next came romance writing—"the hardest and most challenging of all the activities," she confesses.

Books by Emma Darcy

HARLEQUIN PRESENTS

Can you keep a secret?

You can keep this one
plus 4 free novels

Harlequin Presents

Coming Next Month

1007 A DANGEROUS PASSION Jayne Bauling
Their meeting in Nepal brings instant attraction. Only later do their obsessions drive them apart—Grant's for mountain climbing, Renata's against climbing. How can they make a life together?

1008 STREET SONG Ann Charlton
Falling in love just isn't enough. Free-spirited musician Cara and a conservative businessman find their life-styles in no way mesh. Clearly something will have to change—but who and what?

1009 DANCING IN THE DARK Pippa Clarke
There's more to life than work. That's what a successful young journalist discovers when she falls in love with the paper's dynamic new reporter. But love and work sometimes get in each other's way....

1010 THE MARRIAGE DEAL Sara Craven
Reluctantly Ashley agrees the one man to save the family business is her ex-fiancé. Reluctantly she agrees to marry him. It certainly solves the company's problems, but creates personal ones when they fall in love!

1011 SUNSWEPT SUMMER Kathleen O'Brien
Interviewing newspaper magnate Rory Hammond in Palm Beach is a plum assignment, though Lucy takes it to get over the love they'd shared five years ago. Curiously getting mixed up with his current activities gives them a second chance at happiness.

1012 BEWARE OF MARRIED MEN Elizabeth Oldfield
Jorja likes her job in the Cheshire land agent's office yet she leaves when her boss declares his love for her. Past experience made her wary of married men—but the real trouble is she loves him, too!

1013 GIRL IN A GOLDEN BED Anne Weale
An English artist rents a villa in Portofino, Italy, and finds herself sharing the premises with the owner—a wealthy baronet! It's the summer of her dreams—until the lease expires, though not her love.

1014 CHALLENGE Sophie Weston
When Jessica's work throws her into the company of infamous playboy Leandro Volpi, he treats her like a battle to be won. And despite her talent for fending off unwanted overtures from men, Jessica finds Leandro a formidable opponent.

Available in August wherever paperback books are sold, or through Harlequin Reader Service:

In the U.S.
901 Fuhrmann Blvd.
P.O. Box 1397
Buffalo, N.Y. 14240-1397

In Canada
P.O. Box 603
Fort Erie, Ontario
L2A 5X3